T0129409

"Barbara Townsend has in her first novel succeeded in giving voice to the characters in *Under the Wolf Moon* in such a way that they literally speak to you from the page. I eagerly await the possibility of this novel becoming a film. The screenwriter will have little to do in order to bring these characters to life. If you want to enjoy history in a way that is easy and educate yourself on what was not covered in school—this is your read. If you want to feel up close and personal with some of the people who built the all-important infrastructure that made this country—this is your read. If you want to just laugh and cry as you intimately come to know Seamus, Hannah, Granny Sare, and Indian Will—this is your read."

Sandra Madrid Markus,
stage, television, and screen actor.

"Immigrant laborers, fugitive slaves, natives, frontier women, canawlers, railroaders, these are our ancestors! Historian and acclaimed storyteller Barbara Townsend brings them to us with vital detail and tender heart in her novel *Under the Wolf Moon.*"

The Reverend Edward C. Chapman,
Twenty-eighth Rector of historic Emmanuel Church,
Cumberland, Maryland.

"Quick and precise character development and a fast-moving story line make *Under the Wolf Moon* a real page-turner. Barbara Townsend accurately portrays the social, business, and industrial atmosphere in the Potomac Highlands of the nineteenth century. She spins a story that is not only captivating but also historically and geographically correct."

Frank Roleff,
Col. U.S. Army, Ret.,
past President of the Mineral County Historical Society.

Barbara Townsend is a West Virginia award-winning storyteller and preservationist. Shepherd University honored her in the New Writers Fiction Competition for her short story *Dan*, judged by Henry Louis Gates, Jr. The Mineral County Historical Society inducted her into the Order of Crozet, their highest honor given for preservation. She is Curator and Events Coordinator of the Ashby Fort Museum 1755 in the village of Fort Ashby. She lives with her husband and flat-coat retriever on top of a mountain in the Potomac Highlands.

Cover design: Martin Townsend
Cover photo: Barbara Townsend
Author photo: Martin Townsend
Graphic of Celtic knot-work wolf digitized by Martin Townsend from a carving by Clive O' Gibne of County Meath, Ireland

Order copies of UNDER THE WOLF MOON, also available as a recorded book.
Also: a DVD of photographs of sites relevant to the story.

Another great read from Barbara Townsend:
THE CURSE OF THE FROG: TALES FROM AN AGING CHILD, a memoir

More information available on the website: www.the-croft.org

Under the Wolf Moon

A Novel

Barbara Townsend

iUniverse, Inc.
New York   Bloomington

Under the Wolf Moon
A Novel

iUniverse books may be ordered through booksellers or by contacting:

iUniverse
1663 Liberty Drive
Bloomington, IN 47403
www.iuniverse.com
1-800-Authors (1-800-288-4677)

ISBN: 978-1-4502-1338-7 (pbk)
ISBN: 978-1-4502-1337-0 (ebook)

Printed in the United States of America

iUniverse rev. date:3/23/2010

For Martin and Sheryl

At times our own light goes out and is rekindled by a spark from another person. Each of us has cause to think with deep gratitude of those who have lighted the flame within us.

—Albert Schweitzer

I've known rivers:
Ancient, dusky rivers.
My soul has grown deep like the rivers.

—Langston Hughes

Under the Wolf Moon

PROLOGUE

Autumn 2009

The old graveyard is situated on a high knoll barely visible from the road that connects the village of Fort Ashby to Patterson Creek. Weathered slate markers, standing upright, erupt from the earth like teeth and seem to devour the sinking graves. The stones are placed at the head and foot of each. There are no inscriptions and probably never have been. Ancient oak and hickory give bony shade as two women search among the leaves. The elderly farmer who owns the land had a bemused look when asked permission to cross over his field to the burial ground.

"Be sure now, find the special graves, the two long ones with the short one beside." He continued. "It isn't what you'd think."

Ireland's Western Shore
1835

The dock was crowded with people shrouded in woolen shawls as they huddled from the cold wet mist. Seamus was sickened by the thought of leaving. He'd go for now, but he'd return. He had gone down to the sea and raged, shouting his anger into the waves. The salty water splashed over his face as if slapping him in retaliation. Whose fault was it, after all? The dampness only increased his discomfort.

As the water trickled down his face, he remembered blood—crimson rivulets of blood tracking down the bayonets from spiked heads, eyes open, glazed, puzzled by death. Strutting, jeering British soldiers had marched their trophies around the close family neighborhoods, tormenting and challenging all who dared watch.

Seamus was stunned by the faces he recognized. There was Jem, then Davy, people he had grown to respect, County Cork's best hope. They were the ones who promised to fight. They were the ones who would cast out the oppressive Protestants.

Now they glared back from blind eyes like puppet heads on sticks, their lives made into a joke.

Just three short days ago, his uncle Fergal was hanged as an agitator. Anyone related to the Malone family was considered a threat to the British government. On the eve of the hanging, soldiers stormed into their humble cottage and ordered the family outside. They searched their home for guns and hidden rebels. Finding none, they turned the table over, smashed dishes, and ransacked the cottage for valuables.

Two soldiers, with guns pointed at the family, interrogated Padraig and Deidre and their sons, Seamus and Conchuir.

"Bloody hell, where were ya tonight? Did ya see yer uncle dancing at the gallows? Speak up! Give me yer names. They'd best be in English, or we'll shoot you faster than you kin say yer Catholic prayers."

Deidre went first. "I be Eva."

Padraig followed. "Partrick's me name."

"I be James," mumbled Seamus.

"Speak up or you'll not see daylight again," shouted the soldier.

"James be me name," Seamus said as his mouth filled with bile.

"Connor's me name," replied Conchuir. His Gaelic name was so close to the English pronunciation that it mattered little that he said it the usual way.

When they were finally alone, Deidre went to the hearth and removed the loose stone. Bending down, she reached in and pulled out a folded leather pouch.

"'Tis the money and jewelry we have. Enough to pay passage on the ship to America. Pack yer clothes. We'll leave before the sun rises."

Seamus protested. "Our cause is not yet lost. I'm needed here, fer the love of Christ!"

"Sweet Mother of Jesus, we need yer help. Me brother's dead. Do ya need to add yer body to me grief?" cried Deidre.

Padraig caught Seamus' eye. It was clear without another word spoken, they would be leaving together.

Seamus joined his family on the platform as they entered the bowels of the ship, climbing down to the crowded sleeping births where cowards fled to a land called America.

The Cave

The burning embers dimly lit the smooth rock walls of the cave. As the fire flickered, it shone off the dark, bear-greased skin of the Indian. Rawhide and feathers crisscrossed the long dark braids that hung down his chest. He kneeled beside the blackened stone-circled pit. His body rocked back and forth as if he were in pain. In his hands were tightly wrapped bundles of wild hemp and sage. These were placed onto the hot coals until wisps of pungent smoke spiraled up and filled the air.

"Ga-lv-la-di-he-hi, ga-lv-la-di-he-hi, a-yo-tli, ah-yay-la, ah-yay-la ga-lv-la-di-he-hi."

Over and over again, he chanted his tribal incantations until the herbal scents put him into a deep trance.

Next to him, wrapped in a blanket of soft beaver fur, moaned a sallow-faced, dark-haired child. The Indian stood and with his powerful, sinewed arms, lifted the frail girl into the air, high above the swirling smoke.

The Indian implored the Great Heaven Dweller, "*Ah-yay-la, ah-yay-la, ah-yay-la.*"

The smoke carried his prayers into the dark evening. They merged with the howling song of the wolves and rose into the night sky.

Summer
Potomac Highlands
1836

In the muggy night air, the mosquito whined around his face. "Sweet Mother of Jesus," snapped Seamus as he batted the darkness. "'Tis no fuckin' peace even in sleep."

Conchuir stirred in his bed. "Shut up, will ya, Seamus? 'Tis jist a wee bug. Put a blanket over yer head."

"That's the trouble with ya, Conchuir. Nothing ever bothers ya. The little bastard could drain all yer blood and ya'd just lay there a-smilin'," retorted his brother.

"Not true. I'd squash him same as ya. It'd be a bit more pleasant fer me if ya'd quit yer yellin' all the time. 'Tis the rest I need."

"Aye, 'tis the rest we need so we can shovel a hole through the hardscrabble mountain. Ya know what, Conchuir? We're jist beasts of burden fer the Canal Company. Sure enough, the mules have better accommodations. Do ya suppose the boss will let us swap?"

"Go to sleep, for the love of God."

The sun rose over the Green Ridge Mountains, casting a pale orange glow through the thick haze. It was already hot and humid. Acrid smoke clung to the air from the previous day of blasting. It was difficult to breathe, difficult to move. Seamus Malone stretched out his arms and yawned. Before he bent over to fill his water jug from the cool spring, he filled a tin cup with water and poured it over his head. For a moment, the shock of the cold water helped clear his groggy mind. Drinking late into the night was what many of the laborers did. He was no exception.

He shook the water from his hair. Fleetingly, the smoke-filled air reminded him of the peat fires of County Cork. It returned him to a whitewashed rock and thatched-roof cottage, the home he had shared with his parents, and his brother Conchuir. There were people in jaunting carts traveling the twisted lanes, smiles on their faces as they greeted each other. Music filled the evening air accompanied by the smells of warm wheaten bread and mugs of heady dark stout.

It was a romantic vision to be sure. He created it out of his own longing.

"'Tis no blessing upon me soul to be here," Seamus lamented bitterly. "Digging, smashing, shoveling 'tis all I do in this strange land. There's nothing generous here. The soil's rocky, the mountain, 'tis layers of shale, the sea to me home, too damn far away."

He descended the steep steps from the springhouse, turned left, and followed the path down the mountain to the Paw Paw Tunnel. The trail twisted and turned for two miles before it dropped sharply to the excavation site.

Seamus, along with his brother, Conchuir, had signed on as laborers for the Chesapeake and Ohio Canal Company. The work was to dig through a mountain, making the tunnel large enough for canal boats to pass through. Most of the men hired were Irish. Many, like the Malone family, had fled British-dominated Ireland with very few belongings. He knew he was fortunate to have work, but he took little comfort in it.

In the far distance he heard another explosion from black powder. The tarriers had started earlier than usual today.

Seamus grumbled to himself. "'Tis better to die nobly in County Cork fighting fer freedom than being obliterated by razor-sharp chunks of exploded shale. What's the sense in that? Sure now, there's no one in heaven or hell who'd even care."

His irritation increased as he thought how the men were treated. He told any who would listen, "The Company treats us worse than plantation slaves. Because we're not owned, we're cheaply replaced."

"Stick together, men," he implored. "Fer now, this is our meager place in the world. 'Tis what we have. Don't ya see all the cussed German Prots bein' hired? 'Tis our jobs they'll be havin' next. Then where'd ya think ya'll be? Eatin' clods of dirt and sleepin' with no roof over yer heads. 'Tis together we have the power, not alone like a wee bug."

Motivating Seamus was his knowledge of many German immigrants being hired by the Canal Company. He knew they were hard workers as well as damn Protestants. The workforce on the canal could be taken over by them.

Whatever he said, Seamus knew there was no absolute control over the raw, independent spirit of the Irish canawlers. Already mistrust and suspicion had grown between management and laborers, so much so that guards were placed at the excavation site to ensure continued work, to prevent destruction to the tunnel.

It felt like a slap in the face to Seamus that the Canal Company overseers didn't even try to pronounce the Irish names.

There be no getting away from the English even in this country, thought Seamus. "After all, 'twas they who colonized this land. Even now, we're regarded as low as the dirt beneath me feet."

He was known as Shay. In fact, that was better than "Mick" or "Paddy," the names some of his friends were given.

His brother was called "Connor," which suited him just fine. As there was no discernible difference in the sound, it was Conchuir himself who changed the spelling to the English version of his name.

"I don't need to stand out like a blackthorn in any man's flesh. 'Tis not worth the trouble," explained Connor.

Shay was a tall, muscular man with unruly hair the color of dark copper. He tamed it partially by tying it back with a forest-green cord. His full brown beard hung down as far as his collarbone. He looked at the world through green eyes that shifted into different tones according to the color shirt he wore. The eyes slanted downward at the far corners, giving him a deceptively gentle look. In the summer sun his skin tanned to burnished gold, accentuating the startling effect of his eyes.

So much of his appearance fit the description of a Celtic warrior that his family jokingly called him Oisin, the mythic son of the great Fionn mac Cumhaill. All the Irish knew stories about the giant men who roamed their island centuries ago. Mountains with cairns, standing stones in fields, curious rock formations were food for the creative Irish imagination. Their world was alive with mythic heroes.

Despite what many would have agreed were remarkably good looks, Shay felt awkward whenever he saw his reflection. "'Tis me brother, Connor. 'Tis he who got all the good looks what with his hair all black as the coal."

His family, with the exception of his mother, were dark Irish with black hair, black eyes, and stocky builds. While his mother's hair was auburn, she also had dark eyes.

There were stories about the Black Irish descending from the great silkies. The seals would come ashore, change out of their skins, and become human. After seducing and mating with the landed humans, they'd change back into their skins and slide out to sea, later to return to take away their children.

Sometimes Shay would sing in his deep baritone voice a haunting song about the silkie.

> *I am a man upon the land*
> *I am a silkie on the sea*
> *And when I'm far and far frae land,*
> *My home it is in Sule Skerrie.*

As a child he dreamed of being one. Now as a man he simply dreamed of that faraway land.

Whatever caused Shay to believe he was a misfit, it shaped his actions. In the extreme, he felt he had to prove himself worthy of every challenge. He had developed a sharp wit that could cut cruelly. Sometimes it would show up unexpectedly in his quickly ignited temper.

Shay sat on the shaley ground, gently feeling the bruise on his right cheek. His hands were etched with stone dust and dirt, his nails lined in black. The rip in his trousers on the left hip meant that by morning there would be more purple skin.

"Surely now, 'tisn't my fault. The scummer's lazy as a stone and there be already too many around here. He jist caught me when I wasn't lookin'," complained Shay.

"Sure now, it couldn't be yer fault. What with yer red face drippin' with spittle in his, jist shouting about what a miserable disappointment he is to his sainted mother, then turnin' around and asking him to kiss yer arse. How could he be offended?" challenged Connor. "Ya know, Shay, yer yellin' all the time doesn't get ya much. I'm gettin' tired of it."

Connor did understand. He just wasn't willing to give his brother sympathy. It didn't seem healthy. Instilled in Shay was an anger that had been forged into his soul that day in Cork City. It was the nightmare vision that was not a dream: British Protestant soldiers marching with bayonetted heads, his uncle swinging from the gallows rope.

"Connor, for me life I can't rid meself of seeing those murdered men. 'Tis the anger and hatred in me that makes me such a misery. I don't know where to put it," lamented Shay. "'Tis like I don't fit anywhere. 'Tis not here I belong."

"Well now, I be jist as sick as ya from the blood and gore. I try not to think about it. Why should I spend me life rotting me soul with hate? 'Tis that part I'll leave behind. Be careful now, yer temper could kill ya as easily as a bayonet."

Their parents had used up most of the money in the leather pouch, but when they sold the jewelry there was just enough money left for a down payment on a small homestead. Connor and Shay contributed part of their wages to the family farm whenever possible.

Despite his parents' dream of starting a new life in the Alleghenies, Shay desperately wanted to return to his homeland. He couldn't imagine that things were much improved in this place along the banks of the Potomac.

The food, especially in the heat of humid summer, hatched up maggots. He'd pick them out, but a lot of the men didn't bother. Often he'd feel sick after eating the strange stew meat and stale biscuits.

"Where, oh God, are the wheaten bread and the heavy stout?" he'd moan.

In fact, there were times when he did puke and, even worse, have a severe case of diarrhea. His body seemed to be more threatend by the food than anything else on the work site.

The shacks provided for the workers were made from uncured coarse-sawn boards that warped in quick time. The gaps were an invitation to every mosquito, rat, and roach, so it seemed to Shay. Never mind that the rusted tin roof leaked in heavy rain, or that when the snow came, he'd wake with more than his woolen blanket covering him. A man needed a better resting place after picking and shoveling his way through this bleedin' mountain.

Release

Even in the most grim situations, the human spirit seeks moments of pleasure. Some found it in whiskey, others in companionship, and many in both. The two brothers spent as much time together as possible. The age difference between Shay and Connor was less than two years, but Connor's big smile and tousled dark hair made him look much younger. His eyes were the darkest of brown, almost black, trusting and innocent. His nature was gentle and steady, not prone to the outbursts Shay would have. People were drawn to Connor and wary of his brother.

"Connor, ye're so easygoing and good-natured, I don't think ye're paying enough attention to the dangers in life," teased Shay. "Nothing bothers ya. Why do ya never git angry?"

"Ya know ye're angry enough fer us both," responded Connor. "That makes it easy, now, doesn't it?"

Shay took on the task as older brother with great seriousness, much to the amusement of Connor. As different as they were, the bond between them was like ironwood.

After work, on those sweltering days when the rock dust clung to the sweat of their bodies and clogged the nostrils so badly they had to breathe through their mouths, the two would head down to the river. There, they'd strip off their clothes, rinse them in the back eddy at the river's edge, and lay them on the shore's sun-heated rocks to dry.

Picking their way toward the middle of the fast-flowing rapids, the brothers would wedge their naked bodies between the rocks. The cooling water poured over their heads, pounding and massaging every inch of their sore, bruised flesh.

"Listen to this, Shay. I wrote a poem last night. All day it has whirled around me brain. Been tryin' to put a tune to it. Tell me what ya think." As the water roared accompaniment, Connor sang.

> *Let someone love me 'ere I lose what I own*
> *Of time and rest and peacefulness.*
> *Let someone's eye tear with delight*
> *At me coming and me stayin'.*
> *Let someone see me all perfect before them.*
> *God grant the gift of love's chance and love's changin'.*
> *Let me hold fast in the beat of me heart,*
> *Longing for the breath of another,*
> *Whose lips I would caress with me own.*

"For the love of Jesus, Connor, may Mother Mary bless yer romantic soul. I regret to tell ya, 'tisn't going to take first prize at the county fair. Ye're moonin' around like a lovesick cow. There be no girls worthy of such a poem."

"Problem with ya, Shay, ya don't let yer feelings out except when ya punch some poor innocent. Ye're like sweet whiskey in a bottle with a cork so tight ya no can get to it."

When their fingers puckered white, they loosened themselves and shot feet-first down the rapids to the deep pool below. Neither could swim well, but with flailing arms, they raced each other to the rocky shore. Walking upstream in the fading light, the brothers retrieved their clothes and sat on the gnarled roots of an ancient sycamore tree, its white, silvered branches lifting skyward.

"So, Connor, now tell me. What is it that ya miss the most?" challenged Shay.

Connor thought awhile, then responded, "'Tis surprisin'. Not so much the people. It'd be the yellow gorse and purple heather on the hills. The sound of the curlew on the shore, the smell of the peat fires.

"But Blessed St. Bride, I even miss the church. Remember Father Riley? Remember how he made us repeat our prayers twenty times when we skipped instruction? He said the devil would have our souls, but, personally speakin', he seemed to be the devil himself.

"What do ya miss the most?"

Shay had been prepared to speak of friends also, but the longer he thought, the more he realized it was a combination of food and rocks. His stomach grumbled, and he laughed.

"'Tis those hearty stews and the grainy, crusty bread. I miss the peaty taste of spuds, the battered fresh fish, and how the pink salmon flakes when 'tis pulled apart. There's no doubt but I could go on ferever.

"But now to the rocks. Can't eat them, but their power grips me as much as the food. There's a holiness to them. Perhaps they're food fer me soul. Remember when we played in the large circles of stone, climbed into the old tombs, drank from those holy wells?

"Well now, I guess 'tisn't honest if I didn't mention the girls. Ya had the best ones, Connor. You with yer innocent face."

"If I don't say so meself, Shay, many were interested in ya, but yer head was stuck up yer arse. It were the arguments and debates ya liked. I'm not sure ya even noticed the longin' in their eyes."

"Sweet Mother of Jesus, I would now," admitted Shay.

There, while the setting sun cast orange and yellow on the rippling river, they continued to sit on the old sycamore dreaming about growing up in Ireland's west country.

Shay and Connor looked forward to the evenings. On the bluff, overlooking the Potomac, the canawlers had built a stone circle to contain a warming fire of hickory and oak. Set back, around the fire rim, split logs with their rounded bottoms dug into the earth provided adequate seating. As dark descended, men arrived with their allotment of whiskey and gathered around the camp's fire.

On those nights when the moon shone, its light danced and sparkled off the river's rapids. The sound from the distant river was steady and comforting. The whiskey felt good as it washed away the dust from their throats and warmed their bellies. It wasn't long before it produced a false sense of well-being.

The rowdiest men around the fire were the tarriers. They had the most dangerous job at the tunnel site, as they prepared for blasting. Working in teams of two, one would hold a five-foot, double-handled auger upright while the other used the sledge to slam it into the shale rock. Both would then grab the auger arms, twist, and pull the debris up and out. The motions were repeated over and over. Their actions were accompanied by the sounds of clanging metal and deep-chested grunts that reverberated throughout the hills. When the hole was judged deep enough, a tarrier would fill it with black powder and lay a fuse into its opening. Warning cries of blasting would be sounded. All laborers would take cover from the shattering rock. A poorly laid fuse or an ill-timed explosion killed many a novice tarrier.

The muscular, red-mustached tarrier known as Bartholomew was affable and humorous. The men could find no fault in him. They liked him best when he spun colorful tales that made merry of the painful aspects of life on the canal.

Shay knew that Bartholomew had witnessed, in one year, three laborers blown into bloody pieces. Laughing in the face of devil death and ridiculing the Company boss through stories were his way of keeping pain and grim reality at bay.

It was on a summer Friday evening when Bartholomew took a long slug from his whiskey bottle and announced, "I've got a new story to tell if any of you are in the mood for listenin'." The men settled back comfortably in anticipation.

"Now listen here, canawlers, let this be a warn'n. If ye're a tarrier or might want to become one, pay particular attention.

"Old Bill Gough was a tarrier I knew. One of the first to do any blastin' on the tunnel. I was his partner. Knew him to be an honest hardworkin' Irishman.

"The peculiar thing about him were his feet. They were unusually long and as wide as the planks on our shanties. His ears were peculiar too. Hung way down near to his Adam's apple.

"One day we was out blastin', and it was his turn to light the fuse. I was a far distance when he lit it. 'Spect he must have tripped over his great feet, 'cause when the explosion went off, I saw him fly far up into the sky and disappear.

"We looked all over the hills for him, for near half a day. We thought it'd be proper to bury the pieces of such a good man. Couldn't find him anywhere."

Bartholomew reached for his whiskey and filled his mouth with the golden liquid, letting it slowly trickle down his throat. He stretched his sore arm muscles behind his neck and continued.

"It wasn't till late afternoon the next day that we looked up into the sky to see him rapidly descending, his ears flappin' like wings, his large feet paddlin' the air to slow hisself down.

He landed in a thicket of grapevines next to the stream. Hardly a bruise on him.

"Next day we all lined up for our pay. Damned if the Company boss didn't dock a dollar off his wages for the time he was in the air."

Laughter filled the campfire area as more whiskey was passed around. A hoot owl called to another as more logs were added to the fire. Quiet descended upon the men as they stared into the licking flames and dreamed their own private dreams.

During the quiet, Shay began to sing. It was "My Lagan Love," a song he had learned in the port town of Kinsale on the southern coast of County Cork. For him, its minor key captured not just the heart-wrenching love for a woman but that of Ireland herself. *She hath me heart in thrall. No life have I, no liberty, for love is lord of all.* The longing and pain in the words flowed over him, momentarily, as if a lamenting prayer. In the darkness he could allow the tears to fill his eyes.

Later in the evening, Connor stood silhouetted by the waning fire. "I've heard of a magical island off the west coast of Ireland," he said. "'Tis called Tir na n-Og, the Land of the Forever Young. A place where there be no need to work. A place where whiskey and food are free fer the asking. Music from Clairseach, the harp of the Gaels, fills the air. There be no diseases, no agin'. Only warm gentle breezes blow."

Connor hesitated just long enough to let his friends imagine. Then he continued.

"Perhaps most important of all, 'tis where the beautiful Niamh of the Golden Hair lives. 'Tis said that she brought the handsome warrior Oisin to her island on a magical white horse. Together they lived in great happiness until one day, he felt the homesickness fer Ireland.

"Niamh warned Oisin, 'If ya leave, ya must never touch the earth of yer homeland. If ya do, ya'll never will return to me.'

"Oisin promised that he would return to Niamh. Then he leapt upon the white horse and galloped across the waves.

"Ireland looked different to Oisin. People were smaller. Castles had tumbled down, yet beautiful-sounding bells filled the air. Oisin saw two men struggling to remove a boulder from a plowed field. He asked, 'Why are there bells ringin'?'

" 'They're from Padraig's churches,' the men responded.

"Oisin offered to help the men push the boulder out of the way. As he leaned down from his horse, the girth slipped. He fell to the ground. Instantly he turned into an old man. Fer what seemed like a year in Tir na n-Og was actually three hundred.

"The men carried him to the great church where Padraig could be found. It was there that Oisin told the great Saint about Tir na n-Og. 'Tis there that Padraig baptized the ancient warrior before his death."

When Connor ended his story, Bartholomew said, "It'd be pleasin' if there were such an island. But perhaps if we found the magic horse, it might become a wee bit crowded."

Others vowed if ever they had the chance, they'd follow a pretty colleen to the ends of the earth and never even try to come back.

Shay murmered in response, "It'd be a sainted blessin' if life were not so difficult and cruel."

Shay sat back in the shadows feeling a deep sense of foreboding. "Is't all life can offer? Are we trapped ferever like beasts of burden haulin' bits of rock through mud and grime? Livin' from one meager paycheck to another, never to have bigger dreams? Where the hell are the blessed saints in this godforsaken land? Kind Mary, Mother of God, take pity on us. Take pity on me."

It was good that no one could see his brooding. It wouldn't affect the pleasant mood Bartholomew and Connor had created.

Their talk flowed easily to the little people who lived under the ground.

Connor insisted, "Aye, they are real." His eyes grew big as he described seeing them in County Cork when he was a little boy.

"Come on, Connor," responded his close friend Jake "How can you believe in such creatures? Introduce me to one sometime."

Serious discussion among the men continued until even Jake agreed that it was best to say he did believe. If he didn't, it was sure to bring him bad luck. Not that any of the Irish would admit to being in the least superstitious.

Jake changed the conversation by bringing out the fiddle he had carried in an old flour sack. Shay remembered when he first came to the canal. Then, his hands were agile, his fingers worked the strings gracefully. There was no tune too fast for him to play. It was different now. After a year working with the shovel and maul, calluses and muscles had enlarged his hands. They had stiffened up, were no longer flexible.

Jake held up his hands. "Take a look, men. Me hands look and feel like bear paws. The murderous British, the fuckers, forbid the fiddle in me homeland. Now that I have me freedom, me hands are ruined by the work." Trembling with emotion, Jake continued. "I offer me fiddle to anyone who can play it."

There were no takers. Their hands all looked like his.

"Jake, we still have our voices," Shay responded gently. "We can sing. Even better yet, we can protest. Fer as long as we can speak and sing a tune, they haven't bayoneted our souls."

The more the whiskey flowed, the less coherent the words became. No one was sure who landed the first punch, but six of the canawlers joined the scuffle that soon turned into a drunken brawl.

Shay jumped into the middle of the fight and took them all on. He felt a keen sense of exhilaration. His focus was how many men he could pull to the ground, not the demon nightmares.

Troubles

Lee Montgomery, the Canal Company boss, was an unusual man. Shay grudgingly agreed with Connor on that point. Yet there was something about the man that made Shay uneasy.

Montgomery stood six feet one inch, just slightly taller than Shay. He was clean shaven and muscular. His light brown eyes matched the tufts of hair left by his receding hairline, but it was his nose that intrigued the two brothers.

"His nose, 'tis flat. I'd bet me paycheck 'twas a broad fist that made it so," Shay noted.

"Aye, 'tis my belief too. So ya'll not be gettin' me paycheck. He can drink the sweet whiskey with the best of us. I think he could hold his own in a fight, no doubt," responded Connor.

"'Tis said he's a Methodist minister, yet I see no kindness in him. 'Tis said he be respected as a contractor, yet he struts about the worksite like a proud cock makin' the grand promises. Do ya believe what he's sayin'? The Irish crews could be the best around? Do ya trust him?" questioned Shay.

At first the men were hopeful. Then the difficulties of blasting through the shale mountain, cholera, and bankruptcy changed everything. Paychecks came late. Some worried they might not come at all. Work at the tunnel was not going well. Cholera continued to harass the living. The men were angry and fearful of losing their jobs as well as their lives.

Rumors flew around the camp that Montgomery was about to hire stonemasons from Pennsylvania and import British and German miners.

Shay felt threatened. "'Tis the trust he's broken. 'Tis the ocean I crossed to get away from the fuckin' British. I'll not have them or any other Prot takin' me job."

Because Montgomery was aware of the unrest, he continued to have armed guards watching while the Irish crews worked. To Shay it was further evidence that Protestants would never respect Catholic rights.

The nights that Shay looked forward to weren't the same. Instead of camaraderie, violent fights were commonplace. He knew the mountain brew sold to them by the drayman from Oldtown didn't help matters. The Irish called it "potcheen," a homemade liquor that would stand the hairs up on the back of your neck and make you crazy.

When a black-bearded laborer grabbed Jake, threw him to the ground, and began kicking him severely in the ribs, Shay knew things were really different. Never had fights been aimed at maiming their opponent. Maybe a black eye or bruise but nothing more. Shay was always up for a good fight, but now it wasn't the same. There were times when he found himself stepping into the middle of a fight, trying to cool down the anger.

"Sweet Jesus, what do ya think ye're doin'? If ya break yer arm or yer legs, then the company won't have to pay ya. Who's gettin' hurt in all that? Use yer thick skulls. Yer anger's not at each other. Ye're fightin' the wrong ones. 'Tis the devils that rule over us ya should be aimin' yer anger at."

What was beginning to hold his interest, to challenge him, was honing his verbal skills of persuasion and cutting wit. It was more satisfying, something peculiar to him. Shay stood out and had no problem taking on Montgomery when money and safety were at issue. He was winning admiration from the other laborers, even as talk of rebellion grew.

As Shay followed the winding trail down the mountain to the excavation, he mulled over the troubles. As hotheaded as he could be, he knew that being so didn't always get him what he wanted. It felt really good to shout insults in the face of some boorish clod, but the boss had a backbone of iron. He was not someone that could be intimidated.

"'Tis with the reason, not the shoutin'," concluded Shay.

The slope to the left dropped off steeply to the Potomac. Sunlight filtered through oak and hickory leaves and glinted off the pale blue rapids on the river. The scrub pine clinging to the cliffside scented the air. He stopped for a moment, looked toward the river, and breathed in deeply. His senses were filled with the stillness, the heady pine aroma, the etched, variegated blues of the mountains, and the sparkling rapids of the river below. Heaviness left his heart. He knew that this very moment would be the best part of his day.

The rugged path became even more steep and narrow as it dipped toward the tunnel site. In the night, a pine that had tenaciously sent its roots into the shale ground, holding on for many years, finally had lost its grip and fallen across the trail. As Shay stepped over the tree trunk, his foot landed on a round rock. His ankle shifted sideways. White-hot pain shot up his right leg as he fell to the ground.

"Jaysus, me foot, 'tis broken." That in itself was bad enough when, suddenly, he felt something hit his thigh. The impact was followed by a sharp stinging sensation. Slithering down the bank was a thick-bodied copperhead.

It was only seconds that Shay lay there, but it seemed a lot longer as thoughts whirled through his mind. He knew he should look out for snakes especially on the cloudless, hot days of July. It was the time when snakes start shedding, and their eyes film over for a while. Their biggest defense is to strike at any vibration. Copperheads and rattlers were abundant. He had been warned.

"'Tis me fault. I be nothin' but a fuckin' arse," lamented Shay. He held his throbbing leg in the grip of his strong hands. The pressure seemed to help the pain, but it didn't help his heart. It pounded in his chest as a wave of fear passed over him.

The workers had regaled each other with tales of how painful copperhead bites were, how the skin would turn purple, then black as the venom traveled through the blood destroying tissue and nerves, how some even died from internal bleeding.

"'Tis me fate to die from a damn snake in a foreign land, not nobly in me own home country," moaned Shay.

The clatter behind him made his already pounding heart jump. Down the hill came Connor and his friend Jake.

"Hey, Shay, are ya still drunk from last night or did ya trip over yer big feet?" they laughed.

Shay didn't respond, nor did he move from the ground. He just kept pushing on his leg. As they got closer, they saw how pale his face was. It was clear that something was seriously wrong.

Purslane

The walk was long, past the opening of the tunnel, down the mule trail toward the company hospital. Both men supported Shay by his underarms until the mule driver carried him by wagon the rest of the way.

Not much better than the shacks the workers lived in, the hospital was a makeshift building thrown together in 1833 by the on-site carpenters. There had been a cholera epidemic caused by the filthy living conditions in the camp. Hundreds of Irish laborers had died.

Communities like Oldtown fiercely discouraged local doctors from treating sick canawlers and in fact refused to bury the dead in their cemeteries. Uncontrollable fear of cholera had spread to local villages, creating panic. Reports circulated that victims of the disease would turn black and die within twenty-four hours. Those who tried to help often contracted the disease and died as well. It was difficult to find anyone to bury the dead. Bodies were left abandoned in fields and in some cases, mass graves were used to limit exposure.

The labor force in the mines had been getting dangerously depleted, so Lee Montgomery had ordered the hospital built and had established the Purslane Cemetery. The men knew that the word *purslane* was just a fancy word for the invasive succulent commonly referred to as pigweed. It could tolerate poor soil and drought, yet it wasn't much valued.

How bleedin' ironic, thought Shay.

Doc Adams was blunt in size and words. His unkempt gray beard covered most of his face, setting off eyes so dark blue that they seemed to swallow you up like the ocean. Patients did what he said, or they were sent away to cure their own damn selves. Shay's ankle throbbed, but more disconcerting was the deadening ache farther up. His thirst became extreme and his head began to pound.

As he cleaned the wound area, Adams commented, "With a bite like this, no wonder you hurt like hell. Expect some severe swelling and discoloration. It's gonna get worse before it gets better. Snake venom takes some getting used to."

With that stated, he propped Shay up on a cot with a jug of fresh water by his side.

"A big strong guy like you will probably come through this experience just fine, while most of my cholera patients will not. However, it isn't a good idea to step on a copperhead. Your ankle will be fine. It's just a sprain. Stay off it." Then Adams abruptly left.

The pain increased and hung on for days. At times his lips and tongue tingled peculiarly. Breathing seemed more difficult. Time seemed to stand still. Sleep came in pieces as he drifted in and out of consciousness. He thought he saw Connor's face. His bright smile was replaced with a fretful look. The words he spoke were muffled as they rattled around inside Shay's throbbing head.

Doc Adams entered the room and, finding Shay asleep, shook his shoulder gently.

"Shay, ye're doin' okay, but I have a little more work to do on ya before I can send ya back to work. This shot of whiskey might help. First, what I'm aiming to do here is to cut away the dead, blackened flesh from your wound," announced Adams. "After that, I'm going to heat this knife red hot, apply it to cauterize and sanitize the bite area. That's when ya might need the whiskey. If you think it's not doing the trick, then bite down hard on this cloth."

With that said, Doc Adams handed him a small knotted rag. It afforded Shay some comfort when the odor of his own burning flesh reached his nostrils. He felt slightly faint, so he downed the golden liquid, squinted his eyes tightly, and bit down hard on the cloth.

The Tunnel

A few days later, Shay was sent back to work the Paw Paw Tunnel. His right leg felt weak, and he limped.

"Jaysus, 'tis the fuckin' snake. Saints protect me from turnin' into a bumblin' gimp fer the rest of me life," swore Shay.

That morning, the air was still and heavy, made worse from the low-hanging acrid smoke. Again, black powder was being used to blast out large areas of the tunnel. Not only did it reduce falling rock to rubble that was soon hauled out by mule carts, but the vibrations made large sections of the mountain unstable.

There were four shafts being dug and blasted, two from the top of the mountain downward as well as at both entrances. Even with that, making ten feet a week was considered good. The 3,118 feet of tunnel was to be completed in two years. Shay knew work was too far behind to meet the deadline. It was already impossible.

As he walked the trail back to the excavation site, he noticed a natural orchard of pawpaw trees. The tunnel and nearby village received their Indian name from these trees.

They produced a deliciously sweet custardlike fruit unlike anything Shay had ever tasted. He made a mental note of where the largest patches were. He'd come back to gather the fruit in the fall.

Connor whooped when he saw Shay walking toward the excavation site.

"Brother, I see the devil decided not to take ya. There's a good reason. There be work to be done. Since ya decided to step on a snake, life here has taken a turn fer the worse."

Many of the men dropped their picks and shovels and greeted Shay warmly with slaps on the back and rough hugs. It seemed to them that he had come back from the dead. Almost no one these days returned from the Purslane Hospital. But the excitement was about more than that. Work was becoming increasingly dangerous. Paychecks were consistently late and sickness decimated the workforce. Finally the canawlers had their spokesman back.

Connor grabbed Shay's right arm and held it high in the air. "'Tis a man no afraid to stand up to Montgomery and demand what 'tis our due. At last, we might have a chance with the boss," he shouted.

"May the blessed saints shut yer mouth, Connor. Don't ya think that's a bit exaggerated? 'Tis not me who's about to be everybody's savior," said Shay.

Connor just grinned in response.

Montgomery wasn't pleased to have Shay return to the excavation. He knew that man had the persuasive skills of a labor organizer. Yet he couldn't kick him off the job. He was too popular with the Irish laborers.

Rebellion percolated just below the surface. Montgomery couldn't have another work delay. The work site had been sabotaged by an extremist group of discontented laborers. Tunnel supports were weakened allowing debris to fall into the cleared areas. Black powder and tools disappeared. Sickness continued to be a factor. All this caused the forward momentum to slow dramatically. In just a matter of time, new men from Pennsylvania, emphatically not Irish, would arrive, and then the Reverend Pastor could gradually phase out some of the troublesome ones.

Shay wasn't surprised when Montgomery gave him the job of tarrier. Shay had never worked the sledge and auger, never set off black powder. He had watched, with admiration, as the tarriers worked, but he had never wanted to be one. He knew the danger as well as Montgomery. To make matters worse, his partner was Jake, who was also inexperienced, also disliked by the Company boss.

Perhaps luck will be on my side, thought Montgomery, *and an ill-timed blast might wipe out both of the damn Irishmen.*

Shay and Montgomery viewed each other with mistrust. Clearly this was a challenge. Shay was stubborn enough not to step back from it.

The site for the blast was high up the mountain on a precipitous ledge. There was little room to maneuver the auger and sledge. Being the taller of the two, Shay lifted the sledge and forcefully slammed it onto the auger. The ledge felt unstable, and both men feared it might crumble beneath them.

Jake looked up at Shay. "Ya know the devil's tryin' to kill us both."

Shay responded, "'Tis no doubt, Jake, but maybe the mountain will take the bleedin' cur out with us."

After many blows, twisting, and lifting, the shelf amazingly still held. With some relief, Shay filled the hole with black powder. He was determined not to be blown into the air like old Bill Gough. The men carefully laid the fuse and inched their way off the ledge.

Before he lit the fuse, Shay gave the expected warning. "Fire in the hole! Clear out below, lads. Clear the area," he shouted.

All men were alerted to the danger. They moved away from the rockfall slope.

The blast went off with precision, shearing off the unstable ledge.

"'Tis amazing," exclaimed Shay. "'Tis tarriers we be now!"

After the blast had done its job, the canawlers returned to proceed with their work. Connor and his crew were using heavy mauls to break up large chunks of rock, while others shoveled the smaller pieces into the mule wagons.

A rumble, felt more than heard, grew in intensity. As the rock layers split off and gained momentum, the sound became a roar.

At first Shay and Jake were confused. "What's happenin'?" Instantly they knew. Both shouted to the men below, "Danger. Rock slide. Rock slide! Run fer yer lives!" They looked on in fear as the men below scrambled toward safety.

Connor ran for all he was worth. Shay watched breathlessly as his brother was hit midstride, in midbody, by three tons of sharp, fast-moving shale. What was, wasn't anymore. The red ooze of pulverized flesh was all that remained of Connor.

The men were stunned, momentarily still, on the now eerie, silent slope.

Shay felt his stomach twist into a knotted, burning lump. That lump churned and spewed poison to all extremities until his body felt distant and foreign. The wail sounded inhuman, bouncing off the mountain, hammering into the tunnel hole. The primal scream gave voice to horror and guilt.

He slid down the slope, racing to where he had last seen Conner. Rocks continued to fall around him as he began to dig for his brother. The fine rock dust turned the world gray.

"Bleedin', wounded heart of Christ," he sobbed. "Would that I'd be struck blind than see the death of me brother. No, no, not you, Connor. Blessed Mother, let it be me. Let it be me, I beg you."

His friends came and pulled him away from the rocks, took him to the soft, grassy slope. "Shay, we'll collect yer brother. Stay here. Ye're no help."

He fell to the ground and writhed in unconsolable agony, sobbing until his guilted rage and strength gave out.

In the days and weeks that followed, misery sat on his shoulder. It ate away at his soul, emptying him. He wanted no more of himself. But that was not to be. Gradually, Shay began to fill with a profound rage aimed directly at the Canal Company and specifically old Montgomery.

Requital

Many of the villages along the canal were caught in the grip of fear. Disease spread rapidly. Strangers came in great numbers. Hunger and violence were their companions. Resentment and mistrust, on both sides, were prevalent. The people of Oldtown were caught up in this brew and were no exception. As the canal inched toward their village, things began to change.

The people of Oldtown were proud of their ancient history. In the 1700s, it was called King Opessa's Shawanese Town after a lesser chief of the Shawnee Nation. The town was located by a ford in the Potomac River that was used as part of the Great Warrior's Path of the Iroquois Confederation. Later, the frontiersman Thomas Cresap built a stockade fort on the site and set up a trading post. As a young surveyor, George Washington visited him and saw his first Indian war dance. During the French and Indian War, remnants of Braddock's defeated army sought shelter there, as the Shawnee returned to take back their hunting grounds.

Thomas Cresap and his wife had seven children. His oldest son, Daniel, fought in the French and Indian War and settled near a mountain later named for him. Dan's Mountain was a favorite place where he and his friend, a Delaware Indian named Nemacolin, often hunted. His brother, Thomas Jr., was killed, at age twenty-three, by Indians during a skirmish on Savage Mountain. The youngest brother, Michael, led Cresap's Riflemen during the Revolutionary War. His house stood proudly on the main street in Oldtown.

The locals remembered these stories as if they were about kin. Over the years, Oldtown had become a peaceful place to live, proud of its patriotic history.

That was until those foreign Irish started to show up. The canawlers were thought to be the cause of most everything bad. After payday they would arrive like thirsty jackals at the taverns. Fights always broke out and there were gunshots. Some were fired by the Irish and some came from the residents who felt in need of defending their own lives and property.

Jerral Floyd was the drayman who provided whiskey to taverns from Flintstone, Maryland, clear over three ridges to Romney, Virginia. At night he worked as barkeep in the Pine Tavern in Oldtown.

He began his career delivering barrels when he was sixteen. Schooling wasn't for him. He was only good at tallying numbers. It didn't make much sense to him, sitting on a bench, doing reading and writing, when he could be outside making money. Besides, he had developed a strong crush on a barmaid over in the valley.

"Caitlin, Caitlin, my sweet, my love," he'd say over and over in his mind. He had never said anything to her. When he saw her, his tongue seemed to swell up. He could barely blurt out his name.

She was older than he. *All the better*, Jerral thought. *Proves I'm a grown man.* He didn't mind the small wrinkles gathering around her eyes.

He fancied himself quite appealing when she leaned her bosom close to his face to put a glass in front of him. She did flirt with him. She'd toss her red hair and flutter her thick dark lashes. Her Irish brogue was soft with promises.

Many nights he had troubling wet dreams about Caitlin and vowed he would have her as his own. People in Oldtown would envy the likes of him to have captured the heart of such a beauty. They'd live together in the small cottage by the stream and have lots of children to help with his work.

Caitlin led Jerrel to the back room and latched the door. Turning to him, looking directly into his eyes, she said, "Ya do understand what is goin' on. You'll do right by me?"

Jerral's head was muddled with lust. "Of course, Caitlin, I'll do right by ya a thousand times over. I will show you how good I am."

It didn't take long.

As Caitlin adjusted her corset, she said, "Well, now ya can put yer coins on the wee table. The more coins, the more of me there'll be later."

Jerral stopped midway in pulling up his trousers. His head began to throb; spittle foamed around his mouth.

"What?" he yelled in disbelief. "Ye're just a fuckin' whore?"

Again, even louder, he shouted, "Ye're just a fuckin' whore!"

Caitlin despised both words he used. They were demeaning despite the truth in them. It stung. Men did not treat her with such contempt. Yet here was a stupid, scrawny boy shouting at her. Caitlin's temper flared.

"Well, what'd ya think I'd be? Me attracted to a young weasel-faced boy with nothing bigger than a toad's pizzle?"

Her laughter was cruel. "Ya last as long as a popped pimple, ya disgustin' fester upon the land." She continued.

"And further, ya may leave me a jug of yer whiskey. Yer coins won't be enough for me time. Best be generous, or I'll spread tales about yer inferior pecker."

Caitlin left, slamming the door behind her.

Jerral, shaking with humiliation, pulled his trousers to his waist.

He married Clara the following year. She was a plain woman with light brown hair. He wasn't sure what color eyes she had. He didn't pay much attention to her except for his own personal relief. Clara had given birth to a son, which pleased him. Still, she wasn't what he thought he deserved.

Clara will jist have to do. Fer the most part the woman is meek and does what I say. At least there ain't no discussion about toads and pizzles, thought Jerral.

In his mature years, he had put on weight. He was a short, stocky man, whose beard looked as if it couldn't make up its mind. It bristled like a brush in gray and brown. When he laughed, his high-pitched voice sounded forced and uncomfortable.

He couldn't let go of what had happened with Caitlin. After being spurned by her, he nurtured a festering hatred of all Irish. She had indeed spread the story about his inferior body part.

"Hey, Jerral, is it growing yet?" the men would snigger.

Jerral shook his head, trying to rid himself of those badgering memories that made him so angry.

At the tavern one evening, a canawler was stumbling drunk and singing his shanty songs. *No sound is worse*, Jerral thought. It grated on his ears.

When that man appeared in front of Jerral's face and said, "Little man, 'tis another dram I need. Pour it up fast," Jerral flushed hot, and hatred boiled in his bowels.

"Jist a second, fella. I'm gitten' ya the best in the house." Jerral disappeared into the back room and shortly returned with a half-filled glass of warm golden liquid. "Put yer money down. Only the strongest of men can take this. Prove yerself the man ya think ye are."

The Irishman downed the drink in one gulp. Shortly afterward he was out in the bushes puking up the contents of his stomach.

Jerral didn't hesitate to tell anyone who would listen how he had pissed in a glass and sold it for top money to a drunken canawler. It was one of the few times when Jerral, with his high-pitched cackle, would laugh.

His boy was six when Jerral noticed that Clara wasn't feeling well. She had spent a lot of time in the outhouse. Said she had the bad cramps. Finally when her eyes took on the sunken look and her lips began to blacken, Jerral admitted the worst. She had cholera.

"Clara, Clara, ya can't go now. We have a son. I need yer help. I can't raise him by meself. I need ya to raise him till he can help me with the barrels. Ya can't leave me."

Clara thought, *That's the most that man has ever said about me matterin' much.* She felt the haze of death cover her. Blackness took her away.

Jerral wrapped her body in a torn and dirty blanket and grumbled as he threw it into the wagon like an overloaded sack of potatoes. He had heard that the canawlers were dying in such numbers that their bodies were dumped in the field down by the old coal pits.

The closer he came to the field, the stronger the stench. He gagged as he tied his red handkerchief over his mouth and nose. The small field was littered with blackened corpses. He pulled the bundle that was Clara onto the ground, wheeled the mules around, and whipped them into a fast trot toward home.

"The damn Irish brought the disease. They can bury the filthy remains," concluded Jerral. He resented her weakness in subcoming to the Irish plague. As for him, Clara would soon cease being anything more than a dim memory.

He sat in the stiff slatted chair on the porch brooding as night descended. His stomach was in pain from hunger. There was no dinner waiting for him. His boy would have to take that over.

"It's not fair. Other men have strong sons and wives to wait on them. I deserve better."

The boy had watched through the window as his pap had left with his bundeled maw. He prayed that the doctor could fix her, but Pap came back with an empty wagon.

"Pap, where'd ya put me maw? Where'd ya take her?" the boy cried.

"Never mind," his pap said. "What's done is done."

Zebediah Floyd

Zebediah Floyd was nine years old on that summer night in 1838. His head was thatched with unruly straw-colored hair and his bright blue eyes sparkled with curiosity. He was shy and small for his age, something that his pap never let him forget. Nonetheless he tried valiantly to make up for that with courage and practice in any game he played. He was a healthy and normal kid, very much wanting to be like the older boys who hung out in town. In the evenings, Zeb and his friends would sneak out, hide in the shadows, and spy on the men in the tavern.

"I miss my maw somethin' fierce. Maw kept me safe. Sometimes she even stopped the whippin's. One time it was so bad that she git the knife and threatened Pap. He stormed out, not to come back fer three days. Life was good when he was gone. Maw didn't seem to mind. Even sang a purty song into the night." Zeb's face contorted as tears slid down his face.

This mornin', it had been bad. He wished mightily for his maw.

"Zebediah, git over here," shouted Pap. "Be some help. Push them barrels to the wagon."

Zeb struggled with each barrel, pushing with all his might, determined to show Pap how strong he was. The third barrel hit a dip in the ground and twisted sideways, rolling down the hill. Jerral was furious.

"Ye're a little weaklin'. Ain't worth yer weight in food, ya little shit," derided his father.

Jerral slowly unbuckled the belt from around his waist. It was supple, stained dark from the oily sweat of his own body. He snapped it in the air like a bullwhip. Its cracking sound foretold what was to come. He grabbed Zeb by his hair and hauled him to the shed.

"Bend over! I'll make ye a man. There ain't no son of mine be a weaklin'," said Jerral in his high-pitched voice.

The first blow stung like a hive of bees. The second tore into his flesh. The following felt moist and sticky until Zeb lost count and became dizzy from the pain. Lately the whippings came more frequently, yet the boy's resolve grew stronger.

"I ain't never gonna cry. I'm strong. Gonna prove it. Jist ya wait, Pap. I'll show ya I'm the best."

Jerral stopped the lashing, his mouth dry from the exertion. "Ya soon better git strong or ye'll be nothin' more than strips of meat. Ya gotta give me relief with them barrels," he said as he strode off toward the tavern.

Zebediah often felt lonely and scared. Jerral, on the other hand, felt betrayed by Clara, abandoned to fend for both himself and the boy. Repeatedly, Jerral said the Irish were the cause of all their troubles. He blamed everything on them from Zeb's mother's death to the lack of good jobs and even the recent drought.

So it was that the young boy found it easy to think of the Irish as different, not really related to himself, even subhuman.

That summer night, the boys collected a stash of rocks and positioned themselves behind the low bushes not far from the main door of the Pine Tavern. The wind had died down and there was a tenseness in the air. Voices from the tavern became louder and angrier. Scraping noises of wood upon wood and soft thudding sounds punctuated the air.

"Ya guys gotta let me, jist gotta," pleaded Zeb. "I've been practicing. Kin knock a chicken in the head at thirty paces. Killed her dead," he bragged.

The older boys huddled and whispered. "Look, Zeb," said the oldest, "ya kin have the first shot, but our rocks are comin' right behind. Ya git the count of four."

Zeb picked up his special rock, the one with three sharp edges. He cradled it in his hand, warming it for just the right throw.

Inside the tavern, the canawlers became more agitated and belligerent. Old Montgomery was two months late in paying them. Negotiations failed when the company offered to pay twenty-five cents on the dollar. Shay and his men refused to settle for less than what they were owed. Montgomery responded by offering nothing.

"Lads, the boss is a gobshite. He butters his bread with a feather and scrapes it off with a razor," yelled Shay.

Tonight every spare penny was going to be spent on drink, damn his soul. They would hatch a plan of rebellion. Shay still limped, but it did not diminish his formidable strength. His temper was fired up in indignation and his persuasive arguments for confrontation were loud for all to hear.

"Men, listen to me. 'Tis the persuasion we need. If we agree to join together, we'll have the power. We can shut down the work on the canal. There be no strength without unity. The bleedin' devils will have to pay us. We need solidarity," implored Shay.

He didn't carry a gun even though many did. Shay's plan called for verbal intimidation, not ballistic violence. Getting physical toward anyone who threatened to take away their miserable jobs would need careful planning. The time wasn't right.

There were a few others, however, who disagreed.

Jerral had left through the back door of the tavern and stood next to the old wooden shed where he kept his special Irish brew, and he could hear the loud voices coming from the tavern. He noted that the canawler named Shay was stirring up trouble.

His mouth is as fiery as his red hair, Jerral thought to himself. A vision of Caitlin flouncing her red hair and laughing cruelly skittered through his head.

Six men wandered over to the shed, and Jerral became distracted as he sold jar after jar of his watered-down whiskey. He feigned sympathy for their lack of paycheck even though he was determined to glean every last cent from these stupid Irish. He was congratulating himself when he heard the gunshot.

Rage

Zebediah watched as a large black-bearded canawler staggered out the front door. To the four-foot child, the towering six-foot man shouting angrily in an unrecognizable language, waving a long rifle, seemed the devil himself. He embodied all that was bad in the world. Zeb took aim with his three-sided rock and threw with all the might of David fighting Goliath.

The aim was true, landing with a satisfying thud. Everything seemed as if it were happening in slow motion. Zeb saw the rock hit just below the man's left eye and then the blood spurting. The man swung around and the rifle went off. He couldn't have aimed. Coming out into the dark from the lighted tavern, he couldn't have seen the small boy.

The bullet might have ricocheted off the large nearby boulder, but the outcome was that it slammed into Zebediah's head.

As Jerral heard cries for help and his name being yelled, he grudgingly locked his shed door and went to see what had happened.

The rage he felt when he saw his child bleeding and unconscious was white and searing. All that he loved had been taken from him by these alien bastards. His manhood, his wife, and now his son. His fury dug deep into his soul and festered into brooding hatred. And it was this deep hatred that finally aimed at a specific target. It focused on the man called Shay.

It was that redheaded piece of turd who whipped the stupid Micks into a killin' frenzy, thought Jerral. "I'd like to kill them all. Too damn many. They're common as rats."

Jerral vowed, "If the devil gives me the chance, I'll kill that bastard called Shay. He'll suffer. Make sure of that. It ain't right what he an' his kind have done." It was the final straw. Shay symbolized all that poisoned Jerral's soul.

To everyone's amazement, Zeb lived, but Jerral secretly wished him dead. The boy wasn't right. In fact, he couldn't even dress himself. His boyish rambunctious nature was reduced to breathing and swallowing and the most basic of tasks.

Shape-changing

Violence continued to erupt along the canal. At Little Orleans a gang of Irish laborers attacked German workers, burned their shanties, beat and killed a man by throwing him onto a raging fire. Violence at the Paw Paw again shut down work when the new masons and miners arrived from Pennsylvania. Lee Montgomery was forced to use local militia to establish order.

Later in August of 1838, one hundred and thirty men were blacklisted by the Canal Company. Shay Malone was one of them. The list was passed along to all major businesses, including the Baltimore and Ohio Railroad Company, in an attempt to drive troublemakers from the area.

The blacklisted men were dragged like prisoners out of their miserable shacks, marched past the work site, then toward the road. The laborers left behind looked down at the earth, avoiding eye contact. The militia was well armed and not sympathetic toward the blacklisted Irish. Some of the laborers carried their meager belongings in feed sacks on their backs. Shay brought not a thing. There was nothing from his life on the canal he wanted to carry with him.

The people of Oldtown lined the street and waited. With the militia blocking the return road to the Paw Paw, the only choice was to go forward. Someone shouted, "Run for it!" and the men ran the savage gauntlet, pelted by rocks and sticks. Buckets of offal and contents of chamber pots were thrown at them amid the jeers and laughter of the crowd.

Most of the men broke through the line and followed the Braddock Trail toward Cumberland, then west to Ohio. Others split off north, then east, toward the big cities. Only Shay headed toward the Potomac River ford and followed the Warrior's Path toward Greenspring.

His insides churned with anger and humiliation. After Connor's death, it was easy to blame all that was wrong and hurtful on Montgomery. He had thrown himself into the struggle between labor and management with the fury of a madman.

Shay hadn't dared look inside himself. He avoided the dark place that anger filled so well.

Eleven months before, he had gone to his parents' farm with the miserable scrapings of what was left of Connor. The coffined remains were buried on a knoll not far from their cabin. He hadn't told his parents that it was his blast that sent tons of shale slicing into Connor.

He traveled along the winding Indian path, down Broad Hollow toward the Malone farm. His mind was swirling with demons. He felt ashamed of himself as a leader. He couldn't make right the promises to the men he had left behind. To run from anything was not what he did. It didn't fit with how he saw himself. He was angry, enraged, but there was no one to pound except himself.

"I'd rather be going west or east, jist anywhere other than me parents' farm. Disappear, 'tis what I'd like to do."

He muttered to himself, "'Tis County Cork that's callin' me. I'll die as a freedom fighter. Ne'er do I want to see this miserable piece of the world again." Despite his feelings, his legs continued taking him toward the Malone homestead.

Why? 'Tis me need to tell them what I'm planning to do with me life, or is't something else? wondered Shay. *Somehow the choice seems not to be mine.*

If he ever before had felt like an unworthy mutation that didn't fit in the family, that feeling was now magnified a hundredfold.

It was Padraig Malone who recognized the distant figure walking the road toward him. The late afternoon sun was glinting off Shay's copper hair, and the slight limp made it obvious. Padraig could feel the heaviness that burdened his son from afar. It was that powerful. He met Shay on the dirt path to the cabin and put his arm around his shoulders as they walked toward the house. Not a word was spoken.

His mother, Deirdre, was watching from the kitchen window. She was not one to sit quietly, waiting for answers. She often had many strong opinions and really liked giving advice. But there were times when Padraig's dark eyes would pierce through her consciousness and seal her lips. Now was one of those times.

Supper was quiet. The three talked about the usual things, the weather, the crops, when the hogs would be slaughtered.

"Got a boar weighin' 'bout twenty-eight stone. Mean as a cornered wildcat. I'd welcome yer help," said Padraig.

Seamus silently nodded in agreement.

Early that night, Seamus climbed the ladder to the loft and fell into a tossing and fitful sleep. Sharp rocks fell head over end, and he was screaming, but no sound came from his mouth. Then everything turned red like a swirling pool of blood. He'd wake sweating, then fall back into the repetitive dream.

Splitting logs was an effective way to unleash his anger. Each log was given a name, purging the many betrayals that burdened him.

"Montgomery!" he'd shout, and the ax would connect, producing a gratifying sound as the wood shattered in two. "The fuckin' shaley mountain!" *Crack* went the log. "The bleedin' militia. Traitors all!" *Twack*. "Damn cussed snake!" The log split cleanly and fell to the ground. He still limped, which was a constant reminder of that vile reptile.

As the litany was repeated over and over again, that wood pile grew. And as it grew, the dark hold on his soul seemed to loosen its grip. He liked how his mother called him Seamus. It was familiar and soothing. So, to the litany he added the name Shay and hacked away at the bitterness and hardness surrounding his soul.

It wasn't long before Seamus began to notice little things around him. He especially liked the way the long grass blew in the wind, like gentle swells on the ocean. To his surprise, he laughed occasionally. Then the dark would descend, and he would brood over the secret that poisoned his insides.

Finally, one late evening, while he and his parents sat beside the cabin fire, Seamus closed his eyes and said, "'Tis I who lit the fuse. I caused me brother's death."

There was silence. With difficulty, Seamus slowly opened his eyes. He saw the pain wrap around his parents. It was what he feared, that wrenching hurt rubbed raw again.

His mother spoke first. "Seamus, ya can't roll around in yer own misery forever. 'Tisn't something ya could control."

His father added, "I think ya came here to be both Seamus and Connor. You've been neither. We've already lost one son. Kind Jesus, I don't want to lose ya as well. Ya owe us, Seamus."

Tears trickled down Deirdre's lined face. "He has left a hole in me heart that never will be filled. But I know he wouldn't blame ya. Neither will we."

For the first time since Connor's death, Seamus allowed his rage to step aside. His emotions poured out in wrenching sobs.

In the spring when the mountain redbud bloomed, Seamus shaved off his beard and went in search of work. He was hired by the Baltimore and Ohio Railroad Company. The man in charge found no one by the name of Seamus on the blacklist.

Hannah

Hannah Canady first met Seamus when he boldly strolled up to her cabin porch. It was that haunting sweet sound, so reminiscent of bagpipes, that gave him the courage. In the twilight of the evening, the music floated through the air, channeling down the hollows, bouncing off the steep hills. He felt bewitched. Perhaps the fairies had crossed the great sea and found their home here.

Bewitched he was, but it was not by fairies. The woman's hair was a mass of brown curls that fell below her shoulders, her eyes so dark that he felt pulled into their depths. On her lap lay a long box with strings. Her right hand held a turkey quill.

"Please don't stop. 'Tis the music." He grinned self-consciously. "It must have put a spell on me. I didn't mean to intrude." He stood before her like an awkward, shy giant.

She responded with such a warm, broad smile that his heart quivered.

Hannah had seen him before. It was just a glimpse, but unmistakeable. She had walked down to the road's edge to pick wildflowers for her father's bedside. The tall red-haired man with a slight limp had just passed by.

"Have ya never heard a mountain dulcimer before?" she asked. "My father made this fer me when I was but a child. Sit on the step. I'll play you 'Barb'ry Allen.' 'Tis a lovely tune."

Seamus was so moved by the sound, he found himself humming along, his deep voice mixing with the softness of hers.

When she finished playing, she looked up at him. There was that melting smile again. "Let me teach ya the words. Please sing with me."

Their voices floated into the night air, dancing around the melody and chords of the dulcimer, melding together as one.

"May I please come back again, Hannah? I'll sing ya some of me favorites. Perhaps ya'll be able to play them on yer dulcimer."

"Well now, if ya don't come back, I shall be quite sad." She smiled.

As Seamus walked toward the Malone homestead, he felt a lightness in his heart that had been missing for years.

It was no wonder that Seamus was drawn in by the sound of the mountain dulcimer. It was his own kind who had settled in the rugged mountains of Appalachia, who had adapted and loved this simple droning instrument.

And it was no wonder that Seamus and Hannah were drawn together. They complemented each other like the harmonizing strings of her dulcimer. She loved his unruly copper hair, his quirky limp, the hues of his eyes, his fire.

He admired her calm, steady nature that seemed grounded in mystery. She was not predictable. He imagined her to be a silkie and welcomed any spell she might cast.

In 1762 Hannah's grandfather, a Scots Irish Ulsterman, had emigrated from Ireland when he was sixteen. Under British rule, Irishmen who were not members of the Church of England had little opportunity to own land or improve their lives. Other religions could not be practiced freely.

Many who chose to emigrate didn't have money enough for passage. So it was that Hannah's grandfather came as an indentured servant. For seven years he worked for Benjamin Johnson, a plantation owner on Patterson Creek.

Being frugal and hardworking, he eventually managed to purchase land, and a flintlock long rifle with a fine stock of curly maple. By the winter of 1776, he had built a small cabin in Broad Hollow. His dislike for the English had led to his joining Michael Cresap's Riflemen. After the Revolutionary War, he settled into farming and started his family.

His and the next two generations that followed were faithful Presbyterians. By the time Hannah was born in 1820, the cabin had expanded to six rooms with a sitting porch on the front. As Hannah was the youngest of four and unmarried, it fell to her to take care of her sick, widowed father. Consumption was common, and her father was dying because of it.

Seamus courted Hannah in simple ways. He would stop by in the early evening. While sitting on the porch, they would trade songs. Hers from the mountains, tunes of love and tragic death. His freshly from Ireland, filled with the passion of unforgiven wrongs.

As the dim light faded, he would tell her tales of the Fiana, stories of the great Fionn mac Cumhail and his son, Oisin, stories he grew up believing.

Hannah would counter with stories of the great boar that terrorized an entire village and snakes that chased a crazy man named Dan down the road to Patterson Creek. Seamus would shudder and change the subject by singing about the mysterious silkies.

As they sang, laughed, and shared stories from their childhood, a feeling of something more than friendship began to grow, binding them together.

Indian Will

For all he could see, it looked like a dun-colored mound with a pile of turkey feathers on top. Seamus blinked his eyes to clear them. It didn't look quite right to be a turkey. What was that down by the creek? Suddenly it moved and started to grow tall. It was an amazing sight that glared back at Seamus. The face was gnarled and wrinkled like a dried walnut hull. The strong-shaped nose and thin, frowning mouth were set in a face unlike any he had ever seen. Slowly the apparition turned and faded into the forest.

Indian Will knew that man was the "loud one" who had brought a new light to Hannah's eyes. He had seen him coming down the lane toward the cabin. The Indian had chosen to leave quietly by the back door as soon as the herbal drink had calmed the dying man's hacking cough. Lately he came every day to work his medicine on Hannah's father. He knew he couldn't reverse what was to be. He could only ease the suffering. He could pray the man into his white heaven.

The Canady family had no idea how old the Indian was. To Hannah he had always been ancient. Her father had said when he was a young boy, the Indian hadn't looked any different.

When asked his age, Will would raise his hands to the sky and say, "So old the sun was young."

What was true, he had been a trusted friend of the family for generations.

Most of the Indian tribes had left the Potomac region by the late 1700s. They moved farther west, away from the white settlements. Will's family had stayed. At a very young age he had become a trapper and a gatherer of medicinal herbs and roots. When disease struck, it was his medicine that the settlers sought.

Some knew that he lived in a cave but didn't know where. Hannah knew. She knew where to find Will.

As a young child, she had had a fever and cough that grew worse by the day. She became unconscious. Her widowed father, desperate, bundled her in quilts and carried her by mule to the cave high on the mountain ridge overlooking the great Potomac. Hannah was there for days, left in the care of Indian Will.

Sometimes in her dreams at night, she could hear the singsong chanting, taste the warm herbal liquid sliding down her throat. She remembered fear, being lifted high into the swirling smoke, the strong arms steadily holding her and then the soft, comforting fur against her skin.

She was frail when she came down the mountain. But she lived. During those days in the cave, Indian Will began to think of Hannah as his child too. Now with Hannah's father dying, the Indian was the one she turned to again.

Late afternoon when Seamus stopped by for a visit, his green eyes were wide with excitement. "Hannah, darlin', 'tis the most peculiar man I saw down by the old creek. 'Tis an Indian I think he might be."

As he described what he saw, Hannah began to laugh, holding on to her sides from the giddiness she felt.

"Oh, Seamus, he's the most wonderful man. 'Tis he who saved my life. I don't know what I would do without him." Then Hannah told him her story of how many years ago, high in his mountain cave, Indian Will had taken her from near death and healed her.

That evening when Will arrived, Hannah begged him, "Please stay. Meet Seamus. I think he is quite wonderful. Please stay."

Finally he agreed. *Perhaps it would be good to look into this man's eyes. See if his spirit is worthy*, thought the Indian.

When they did meet, it was Indian Will's hat that most fascinated Seamus. He could barely take his eyes away from it, partly because the Indian was glaring at him. His stare was so direct, he didn't know how to respond. The hat was easier to look at. *'Tis a most amazing hat*, thought Seamus.

In return, Will's eyes shifted to the mass of copper hair on the Irishman. *Scalp worth much money*, mused Will. He wondered how much the French would have paid for the likes of that.

Hannah looked on in dismay. Could these two very different men learn to trust each other? Even be cordial? Her heart began to sink to her stomach.

The Indian was aware of her feelings and thoughts. He could be miles away and know. Slowly he made the first offering of friendship. The wise Indian handed Seamus his hat to hold. It was made of an ash splint frame, covered in deer hide, topped with a circling array of splendid turkey feathers. Around the edge were porcupine quills cut in different sizes and sewn on as decoration. Chiefs of the Iroquois Nation wore a similar headdress that included deer antlers. It was called a *kastoweh*.

Turning the hat gently in his hands, Seamus realized, *'Tis me he is trusting. It be precious in me hands. 'Tis not offered to jist anyone to hold.*

Assumptions

Hannah knew. Early on, she knew but said nothing. Seamus was Catholic. It wasn't true she thought of him only as a friend. There was a lot more to it than that. Even if it had been only friendship, that would have pushed the limits of what was acceptable. The Scots Irish Presbyterians stayed pretty much to themselves, bartering with others for goods but not much else. The fact was, she was lonely. The other fact was, she really liked him. Love just wasn't possible. She knew that it couldn't lead anywhere. Perhaps these strange feelings would fade. She had hoped to wake up one morning to discover he was a boring lout.

Seamus, on the other hand, was full of assumptions. He had told her about his uncle being hanged, the bayoneted heads, his hunger to return and fight for freedom. He didn't need to use the word *Catholic*. Everyone knew the faith of the Irish immigrants. His warmth for Hannah blurred what was not said. Knowing her family came from Ireland made them the same. It didn't occur to him that she might believe differently.

The late summer afternoon was so hot and humid it reminded Seamus of the suffocating air that often hung around the Paw Paw Tunnel. Any thought of those days put him in a testy mood. He wasn't about to tell Hannah that part of his life.

Hannah seemed distracted. Death continued to torment her father. He would come so close to dying, only to improve the next day. It was just enough to give her hope in a miracle. But today was worse than bad.

"Seamus, I think I need Reverend MacIntyre to come."

Seamus felt jolted. "Don't ya mean Father McCauley?"

If someone could explode from within, Seamus did. His face turned red and contorted. The words flew from his mouth and were aimed at Hannah. So stunned was she by his fury, that she couldn't, wouldn't hear most of what he said.

Seamus felt led on, made foolish, lured into giving his heart to someone who could never be his. He felt the anger fill up the frightened space inside him, and the words kept coming.

"Mother of God, Hannah, ya have bewitched me. Ya know our kind can ne'er mix. Ya have lied to me by pretending to be me friend. I told you what happened to me friends, me uncle. 'Tis yer kind that continues to destroy Ireland. Ya have played with me affections like a cat with a mouse. By all the saints, ya have betrayed me."

It took a lot for Hannah's temper to flare. But facing her was a huge, red-faced man totally absorbed in himself, showing no consideration of what she was going through. Her verbal assault on Seamus was equal to any he had ever unleashed.

"You are the one who came to my cabin porch all charm and smiles. 'Tis you who assumed all the wrong things. Ya didn't ask the right questions. Ya didn't want to know. You are so full of yerself that my stomach turns. Ya have no compassion for anyone other than yerself. My father is dyin'. That is what

I care about, not you. Ya are the most self-absorbed man God has ever put on this earth."

Her eyes darkened and calmly she pointed to the lane. "Get yer big feet to carry ya off my land. Don't come back."

The Railroad

For as long as Seamus stayed angry at Hannah, he could cover up the loss he felt. He found himself working longer hours laying down track. Sometimes he would even stay on-site ready for an early start the next morning.

The workforce was made up of mostly Irish and Germans, a feisty combination to say the least. He had worked hard to keep a low profile among the men, but since his fight with Hannah, his biting wit came back with a vengeance. He irritated a lot of the men, especially the Protestant Germans. Any chance he got was turned into an opportunity to prove his worth over theirs.

If a rail tie was misplaced, he'd say, "Now, look here, 'tis the work of the bumblin' German Prots. Can't even measure. Dumb as chunks of wood, I say." If a German crew took a break, Seamus would deride them. "Ye're no better than the disgusting Brits, leavin' it to others to do the work." He felt miserable inside himself, and that misery oozed out like venom onto anyone slightly different than himself.

It wasn't long before a fight broke out between Seamus and a German named Conrad.

"It's yer mouth I'd like to shut permanently, ya dumb Mick," shouted Conrad.

"We be evenly matched. 'Tis beatin' the lard out of ya, I'll welcome. Ya stupid Prot," Seamus hotly replied.

The laborers took sides, cheering on their favorite man. Each was landing solid punches. It looked to the onlookers that it would be a fine fight.

Seamus was surprised when a forceful blow landed squarely on his jaw, sending him sprawling backward onto the gravel. Over him loomed the six-foot-four-inch, two-hundred-and-seventy-pound foreman named Eckhart. Seamus had seen the foreman wade into a brawl with a wooden cudgel and quickly bring peace to the situation. He was grateful that it was his fist this time, not a club, that had hit him.

Eckhart wasn't just convincing physically. He was wily and bright as well.

The foreman handed the Irishman a one-hundred-pound maul and said, "Seamus, haul this over to that damaged rail." He pointed to one that had a serious bend in it. "Use the maul and straighten it out," he instructed.

Seamus struggled with that maul, nearly crashing it down on his leg several times. When exhaustion set in, Eckhart picked up the tool as if it were a forty-pounder. He slammed it onto the bent rail. Three times, and it was straightened.

Eckhart said, "There, if you want to challenge someone, I'm it. Until then, I expect you to use your mouth for the good. Stop fights. Don't start them."

Seamus sat around the campfire after most of the men had gone to sleep. He massaged his bruised jaw and thought of all that had happened during the past month. He was honest enough with himself to admit most of his anger was rooted in his fight with Hannah.

"'Tis not all Protestants worthy of me hate. Ya really can't tell a Protestant from a Catholic if ya don't know. Here they don't march around with heads on bayonets."

He remembered Connor asking, "Why do ya spend yer life rotting yer soul with hate?" Warning him that his temper could kill him as easily as a sword.

Gradually Seamus softened, his anger dissipated. Eckart had offered a challenge. "Use your mouth for good," he had said.

Building on his experience at the Paw Paw Tunnel, Seamus became so skillful with words that many a fight lost its momentum. Instead of biting wit, he used his persuasive Irish humor.

"'Tis I who could use yer help now lifting this rail. It might drop on me foot. 'Tis a limp I've got on one side. Saints preserve me from havin' it on the other."

At first the Germans were not trusting of such a change, but when Seamus made himself the object of the jokes, they started to relax a bit.

Eckhart and Seamus began to work well together. Morale improved, and gradually the crew became efficient. It was clear that the railroad would get to Cumberland long before the canal.

Hannah's Grief

The winter came, painting hoary frost on the ground. The cold and dark were all that Hannah could feel as she sat in a death vigil by her father's bed. She willed each breath to be his last. He had begged her to end his misery. And when he was too weak to talk, his eyes implored her. She heard him only too well.

Quietly she said, "I can't."

Over and over again he pleaded.

"Father, I can't."

Finally he turned his head away from her and tunneled deep into his spiraling death.

It was Indian Will who came each evening. He chanted his prayers, burned herbs, and gave her father quieting drink. For Hannah, he brought rabbits, squirrels, and roots to nourish her body, firewood to warm her cabin. She knew that he held her center together, kept her from shattering.

It wasn't only her father who dug painful holes in Hannah's soul. Through her sorrow emerged a longing, and her thoughts unwillingly returned to Seamus. She was so tired, and yet the nights tormented her. In her dreams she would see him smile and then rage. His words fell gentle, then hurtful. With the confusion came the desire to see him again. But then again, maybe not. She needed no more pain.

Hannah was determined to be with her father the very moment he died. Lifting her father's hand in hers, she thought his skin felt like thin, flexible parchment. The veins looked like high blue rivers as they carried his flowing blood. On the side of his wrist, she felt his pulse beat steadily, hesitate, then beat on. These were the same hands that had been strong as hickory in her youth, rough from felling trees, clearing brush, planing wood; the same hands that tenderly laid her mother in the coffin, disciplined her when she sassed, and comforted her in times of sadness. Now they were so cool and smooth, so frail.

She held his hand gently against her cheek and kissed it lightly. She would hold on for as long as it took, holding him while he died. She would be the strength for him as he crossed over and entered heaven. Perhaps then he would forgive her for not doing his bidding.

Food had not been on her mind. It was only when she felt a sudden hunger pang that she realized she had not eaten since yesterday afternoon.

'Tisn't wise, thought Hannah, *to starve myself.*

She let go of her father's hand and hurried to the pantry for a thick slice of wheaten bread. When she returned, her father was dead. Hannah was devastated and cried out her guilt.

"I am a selfish, wretched person. I should never have left his side," she wailed.

Indian Will placed his hand on her shoulder as she sobbed. He said quietly, "It was the only way. You had to let go."

The crisp night air mingled with the scent of wood smoke as Seamus turned down Broad Hollow. He always dreaded going past the lane that led to Hannah's cabin. His heart willed him to turn, but his pride stubbornly propelled him straight on. The crescent moon dimly lit the road, allowing a familiar shape to be seen coming toward him. It was the hat with feathers on top that identified the shape as Will. The Indian had no problem in recognizing Seamus, what with his size and quirky walk.

Seamus' heart quickened at possible news of Hannah. The two men talked briefly and then parted. The closer to the lane he got, the faster his heart beat. Even his legs felt unsteady. He knew she was all alone. He certainly knew something about grief. The thought of Connor's death punched at his insides. Perhaps some of his pain could absorb some of hers. Perhaps she won't tell him to go away. If she did, he'd try to understand. His heart willed his legs to turn down the lane and his pride, at least for the moment, was set aside.

Seamus knocked softly on the cabin door and waited, holding his breath. Slowly the door opened, and Hannah stood in front of him in the dim firelight. To Seamus, she looked fragile, vulnerable in her grief.

He took her by the hand and said, "Hannah, I've missed ya most terrible. May we go out by the old linden tree? 'Tis something I've never told ya. 'Tis the pain I carry about me brother's death."

Gently he led her down the porch steps toward the ancient tree. They sat on the hickory bench that her father had made, sat close but not touching, as Seamus poured out his story of Connor and the details of how he had died. Seamus had spoken of it but once to his parents. There were times when his throat constricted and words could barely escape, but he continued.

Finally he said, "When someone ya love dies, the love still remains. Sometimes the hurt and suffering can numb us to our bones. We want to bury the love and memories right along with the body. 'Tis what I wanted to do, but I swear by Mother Mary, it hasn't brought me happiness."

Gently he held her and said, "Look at the moon. 'Tis the new one holding the old in its arms. Many times I watched as ya held yer father in jist such a way."

When Hannah was a child, Indian Will had taught her that each month the moon was given a different name. This was January. Above was the Wolf Moon, reflecting back the truth she already knew about mortality.

As they walked back to the warmth of the cabin, Seamus said, "'Tis more talk we need, but later will be better."

"Yes, I will want to," agreed Hannah. "Right now, 'tis so very tired I feel."

He pulled her gently to him, led her to the four-poster bed, and held her in his arms throughout the night. For the first time, in so long, she slept soundly.

The Burial

The funeral took place high on a knoll overlooking Patterson Creek. Before the knoll had become a cemetery, it had been a favorite campsite of the Shawnee Indians. During the French and Indian War, they had gathered there to plan raids on the plantations and defensive forts in the area.

The remnants of an old fort situated between the knoll and the creek could still be seen. It had been one of sixty-nine forts ordered by George Washington in 1755 to be built to protect the settlers during the war. The colorful Captain Ashby had come close to losing his scalp after wandering away from the fort without protection. He narrowly escaped the Indians who were waiting for such an opportunity.

Most of the villagers knew stories about the Indian attacks. Some of their distant relatives had been scalped, their plantations burned. Hostility toward Indians in general was deep-seated.

Indian Will chose not to come to the funeral. He had already said his farewell. When Hannah's father died, the Indian went to her fireplace, sat on the floor, and took out charred bits of wood. He rubbed the pieces between his fingers and then darkened his face in grief. He lit small bundles of hemp and sweetgrass. As smoke began to spirial, he went to the dead man. He waved the burning herbs over the body, chanting the released soul onward in its journey to the Great Spirit.

Minutes before Reverend John MacIntyre began the somber burial service, Hannah was joined by her two sisters. The Hagerstown-Baltimore train had arrived late, and she was greatly relieved to see them. They held each other close in a tight huddle near the open grave. Hannah, dressed in a long black cloak that had belonged to her father, looked tiny and fragile under its weight. She trembled, but it was not from the cool air. It was from the barren loneliness she felt.

Somehow, thought Hannah, *I'll put meself back together. 'Tis the love father gave me fer so many years, I need to share. 'Tis a dishonor to father to just crumble to pieces.*

As the minister repeated comforting words from the Holy Bible, Hannah felt a warmth tingle through her veins. Her shaking stopped, but still that empty feeling inside her remained.

Seamus did come to the funeral, but he stayed on the far edges of the small gathering. He thought it odd that there had been no wake.

Catholics really know how to send a man on his way. These Protestants seem overly glum. 'Tis confusing. 'Tis not how I experience Hannah, mused Seamus.

Hannah's sisters had taken notice of the handsome copper-haired man. "'Tis a fine young Irishman who's takin' notice of ya," commented her sister Leah.

Hannah just smiled in response.

Of course nothing was said about his being Catholic.

Possibililties

Weeks passed before Hannah felt the numb, dull feeling of loss loosen its grip on her life. She began weaving again. The rhythm of the shuttle and her feet on the treadles brought a soothing cadence to her being. The forceful beating of threads with the reed expelled pain and gave release.

She placed her dulcimer on the old plank table, instead of tucking it in the corner of her bedroom. Whenever she walked by, she'd pick it up. First to caress it, then to pluck a string. Finally it again became her friend. She couldn't play it during the last month of her father's dying, but now, ever so gradually, the tunes changed from mournful and sad ballads to lighthearted jigs.

It was Seamus who also helped. When he came to see her, her heavy heart packed up and left.

It wasn't long before Seamus brought up the subject of their differences. Neither of them wanted to disturb their fragile relationship, yet both knew it was necessary. It helped that he began by apologizing for his rudeness and anger of months past.

"Sometimes 'tis me temper that takes over. Then me mouth doesn't say what's in me heart. 'Tis me prayer that you and the blessed saints will forgive me. There be only the kind thoughts I have fer ya."

"Seamus, I do forgive ya. 'Tis the truth, I have really missed yer stoppin' by."

There was a long, awkward pause.

Then, fearing the ground might collapse under him, Seamus said, "'Tis a Catholic, I be. I can't be anything else."

Hannah sat silently.

Finally she said, "Seamus, I can't become a Catholic."

And so they sat side by side, smarting from the truth they had acknowledged.

There was a place inside herself that Hannah went in times of distress. She dug around and pulled out an idea.

"Often, Seamus, 'tis time that is needed. Let's wait until fall. If we are still feelin' the same way fer each other, then we can talk about this again."

Seamus jumped at the idea. Both secretly felt that, in time, the other might change.

Spring Passages

The spring rains came, washing away the last vestiges of snow. Bluebirds searched for nesting places and the air was punctuated by feathered wings and birdsong, each to its own. Storms were heralded by the distinctive rapid staccato sound of the mountain cuckoo. Redbud, wild dogwood, and serviceberry trees brought bursts of color, accenting the pale soft green of new leaves. In the evenings, peepers and bullfrogs added to the chorus of night sounds.

With spring came a lifting of spirit; for Hannah, a shedding of winter's gloomy darkness and grief; for Seamus, a dizzying light-headedness much better than the effects of strong potcheen. Together they could feel the earth coming alive beneath them.

Earthworms left their castings, and even before the flowering trees began their spectacular show, the pungent ramps appeared as harbingers of yet another Appalachian spring.

With her hickory-split basket on one arm and his hand in her other, Hannah led Seamus to the base of Valley Mountain.

There, among rocks and bare trees, was a large patch of green leaves poking above the dead debris of winter.

Seamus smelled the ramps' overly strong scent. "'Tis a terrible strong smell. 'Tis beyond me imaginin' that they be appetizing."

But Hannah smiled her big smile and Seamus' heart danced as they filled their basket full.

Back at the cabin, Hannah set about managing the conversion of Seamus. He would just love the ramps by the end of the day. She was sure.

He was sent out the door to gather six eggs from the henhouse and a few potatoes from the root cellar. She made the corn bread, set it to bake by the fire, and began to fry a whole mess of ramps in bacon grease. The odor was so strong, her eyes stung. When Seamus walked through the door, the strong, pungent smell hit him squarely in the face. It was worse than he had expected. With teary eyes, Hannah laughed and gave him that smile again.

"I promise it'll grow hair on your chest," she said.

He grinned back and said, "Hannah, darlin', I already have plenty."

She had noticed the curly hairs poking out around his collar. She felt a peculiar stirring deep inside her body.

They ate the fried potatoes, eggs, corn bread, and bacon-flavored ramps on the front porch, in part to get away from the smell but also to take in the warmth of a sunny spring afternoon. Seamus ate everything on his plate, even had a second helping of ramps. Afterward he leaned over their plates and breathed his garlic breath onto Hannah's face.

"Hannah, darlin', I think I can do this jist once a year."

Hannah breathed back and kissed him gently on the lips. That kiss so tingled their insides and dizzied their heads that the reeking ramps smelled like sweet spring. Indeed, they continued to kiss until their bodies trembled.

Seamus rose from the table and pulled her upright. He nuzzled her neck, bent down, and kissed her breasts through the cloth of her blue-flowered shift. In turn, she undid his shirt, one button at a time, and placed her hand on his chest, stroking the burnished hairs. Standing in the sunlight of the spring afternoon, they marveled at the beauty of each other.

Their courtship was like an adventure game. They tried taking turns, but mostly it was Hannah who had the ideas. She knew the terrain, and Seamus was willing to go anywhere with her especially if it had to do with food.

When the wild blue violets bloomed, the serviceberry flowered, and oak leaves were the size of mouse ears, the two headed toward Valley Mountain.

"'Tis the morel that is the most delicious mushroom God ever created," Hannah insisted.

It was easy to identify the cone-shaped, honeycombed delicacy. Its earthy, woodsy smell would please Seamus more than the stinky ramps.

She led him over the first ridge, then to the base of White Horse Mountain to a place called Swisher Hollow. Hannah remembered coming there with her father, to the place of sycamore trees and damp earth. At first she saw nothing, but soon her eyes acclimated to the hunt. Seamus was quick to catch on. They each whooped and hollered when they found their prey.

It was Seamus who found the ten-inch-high morel. It stood on the forest floor like an Irish fairy house.

"Hannah, darlin', 'tisn't a good idea to pick it. 'Tis bad luck to anger the wee people."

The look that Hannah gave him made him quickly pluck it from the ground. With their baskets packed full, they headed back.

It was another rite of spring accomplished, and they looked forward to the reward.

"Seamus, ya found the prize morel, so ya win the honor of cookin'. 'Tis simple. I'll show ya how."

They built the hearth fire while the morels soaked in a bucket of salt water. Using two large cast-iron skillets, they quickly fried the mushrooms in fresh butter. Dinner consisted of nothing more than just platefuls of morels.

"'Twas a fine cookin' lesson, dear Hannah," said Seamus as he leaned toward her to showed his appreciation with a lingering kiss.

It was a dangerous thing to do, this kissing. Both were raised with the belief that conjugal behavior belonged to marriage. Their bodies, however, seemed not to care. Boundaries grew softer.

Seamus picked her up and carried her to the walnut poster bed. This time he removed her shoes. Beginning with her toes, he nibbled and stroked her body all the way up to her welcoming mouth. They touched each other through their clothing, exploring contours, folds, the soft and warm mysterious places.

The agony of incomplete love left them with a hunger for each other that kept growing stronger. They lay there, wrapped tightly in each other's arms, as if holding on for dear life.

It was clear to both of them that it would be a long, hot summer.

There were many days when they didn't see each other. The railroad kept Seamus working steadily most of the time. Truth to say, his mind wasn't always on his task, but he was very easy to get along with. His mind often drifted to thoughts of Hannah.

'Tis her soft touch on me skin that gives me shivers. 'Twould be a blessin' to be her prisoner, bound to the sweet earth with her kisses, havin' her naked body caress mine.

Momentarily, his mind shook loose from the fantasy. *May the saints protect me from others readin' me mind. 'Twould be an embarrassement fer others to know what I be thinkin'*, thought Seamus.

But soon he would return to his dreams, following them to scenes that made color rise to his face. She was unsettling.

Hannah was no better. At night she wanted him next to her, and she didn't want clothes in the way either. He was so unsettling.

Whistle Pig

The groundhog lay dead on Hannah's pine plank table. Seamus said he had a surprise.

Her eyes snapped at him. "What kind of surprise is that? 'Tis a whistle pig like any other."

"I promise ya, by me blessed saints, 'tis special," he said. "The surprise is not now but fer later. Fer tonight, I was hopin', Hannah, darlin', you'd cook it into a stew."

What is it about men, thought Hannah, *that food is so important? He greets me with a carcass first, then a hug second.*

She frowned. "Well, first ya gut it, skin it, and take the head off. Then maybe you'll get yer stew."

Seamus grinned. He loved to irritate her slightly, not to the point of anger, just enough to see her toss her thick brown hair and flash her eyes. There was something about being combative that engaged his senses. Not that his senses needed a whole lot of extra stimulation these days.

Seamus was secretly excited about the surprise. He really had meant "not now but fer later." It would take a few weeks.

The groundhog was delivered accordingly, and then Seamus left with the ash hopper. He carefully took the skinned and scraped hide, placed ashes on the flesh side, and added enough water to saturate it. In about four days the fur would be easily removed.

He placed the hide in the wood shop where Hannah's father had built her dulcimer. Seamus paused and looked at the old tools, handles worn smooth to a warm glow. He picked up a coffin plane. The iron blade had been kept meticulously sharp. It felt good in his hands. Hannah's father had lovingly held and worked with these tools, building shapes that grew into music. Seamus loved her dulcimer and wanted so much to make music with her. Their voices mingled well, but that wasn't enough for him.

He took a wide split of green hickory and fashioned it into a circular hoop to dry. When it was ready, he'd finish the work.

Seamus returned to the cabin. "Hannah, darlin', the surprise I have for you will take a while. Will ya be promisin' me to stay out of yer father's wood shop?"

Curiosity was heightened in Hannah, but she gave her word. Both knew it wouldn't be broken.

A few weeks later, in the cool of a summer evening, Seamus left the wood shop. He was pleased. The sound of Hannah's dulcimer floated through the night air. He held the surprise behind his back as he walked up the porch steps.

"Close yer eyes tight, Hannah, darlin'."

Along with the night sound of peepers and crickets came a soft heartbeat that grew ever so steadily into a driving, insistent rhythm. Hannah's pulse quickened and her eyes opened to behold a strange, circular drum. Seamus had just introduced her to the Irish bodhran.

Into the evening they experimented, blending the old Appalachian tunes with those from a green island far away.

White Horse Mountain

The leaves began to turn red and gold, adding brilliant color to the mountains. Instead of bringing delight to Hannah and Seamus, the leaf change brought a feeling of dread. They had made a pact to speak again of their differences when fall arrived. The only change that had occurred was now they were totally and helplessly in love.

Both held stubbornly to their church heritage. It was a fact. Seamus would always be a Catholic and Hannah would always be a Presbyterian. From an early age they had been steeped in their traditions. It would be dishonest to change, even for love.

So it was that, when Indian Will came by with an early fall supply of roots and herbs, he found them sitting motionless, side by side, on the porch steps. Hannah's eyes were teary, and Seamus' were dark and brooding.

Will hunkered down in front of them and waited. After a long silence Hannah spoke first.

"Oh, Will, me heart, 'tis in misery. Seamus is Catholic. I be Presbyterian. We cannot be other than what we are. We cannot agree."

Seamus added, "'Tis our churches. They be so different. We cannot be unfaithful to our God."

As they poured out their pain, they spoke of irreconcilable differences, spoke of their warring gods and sadness.

The Indian sat silently. He felt as though he were presiding over a tribal council.

In his role as chief, his words of wisdom were needed. He loved Hannah and increasingly was growing fond of Seamus. The old Indian was puzzled that they attributed so much divisiveness to their God.

His words were brief. "There is one Great Father looking down on us all. We are all the children of God. The sun, the darkness, the winds are all listening to what we have to say." Then Indian Will quietly left.

Seamus reached for Hannah's hand. She responded by putting her hand gently in his.

"Seamus, would ya be willin' to take yet another long walk with me? There's a place on top of White Horse Mountain. 'Tis sacred to the Indians. They believe 'tis where the Great Spirit is close. They go there to seek wisdom and to speak with the spirits. Will ya please come?"

What Hannah described sounded familiar to Seamus. When he was a young boy in Ireland, his family would go on a prayer journey once a year. They would walk to the high peak of a mountain, to a holy well, or to the remains of a stone hut where a Celtic monk had dwelled.

In these places, he had felt a palpable closeness to God and the holy ones. The Irish called it a "thin place"; maybe this was such a place.

They packed a small lunch and began what Seamus termed a pilgrimage.

It was a steep climb up White Horse Mountain. The mountainside was treed with oak, hickory, and walnut. Small boulders littered the slope, yet Hannah seemed to follow a trail invisible to Seamus. They were almost to the summit, when Hannah stopped and pulled a long cloth from her basket.

"Seamus, ya must trust me. I want to surprise ya with something special."

With the cloth placed over his eyes, Seamus totally gave himself over to her guidance. She led him gently around rocks and over limbs until they reached the place. As she removed the cloth, what Seamus saw was a glistening white rock. The right side rose eight feet into the air and formed what looked undeniably like the head of a horse. The boulder extended behind the head to form a long, flat, shelving rock.

They pulled themselves up onto the flattened part where they were met with a breathtaking view. There to the east, the vast wilderness mountains rolled one after the other. Straight down the long slope of White Horse Mountain flowed the snaking waters of the great Potomac.

They sat for a long time on the rock, sometimes staring into the mountains, other times with eyes closed, silently praying their prayers. Perhaps the sacred rock spoke to them. Perhaps the one God reached through the thin place and touched their hearts and minds.

Quietly, Seamus said, "Hannah, darlin', 'tis one thing I know. Sweet Mother of God, I want ya to marry me. To be sure, I don't know how, but will ya?"

Slowly, she replied, "Seamus, I will marry ya, and I think I know how."

He placed his hand on her back and drew her near. Seamus gently removed her shift, his shirt and trousers, their underclothes, and made a soft bed. Their hands trembled as they carressed each other. He carressed her long, dark hair, the elegant neck, down to her silky breasts. She carressed his strong jawline, the muscles, down to his belly. Down, down, their hands slid, his feeling her soft curves, hers, his taut thighs. Their limbs entwined.

Hannah's hand reached for the part of him that grew under her touch. He responded and entered the warm dampness of her. Their hips came together, undulating until all their pent-up desires were unleashed, their bodies wildly exploding into ecstasy. Seamus was convinced he had reached heaven. Hannah lay stunned by the powerful beauty of it all.

The gentle breeze from the mountains murmured its blessing.

Marriage
1841

Father McCauley, of St. Patrick's Church, Cumberland, Maryland, was pleased to marry such a comely twosome. Fine children they'd have for sure. He assumed that Seamus had very recently arrived from Ireland. His Irish accent bespoke that. He probably fled from the troubles like so many good Catholics. As for Hannah, she was such a fine Irish girl from the Irish Canady clan. Poor young thing, all alone in the world except for the ancient Indian called Will.

Hannah wore her mother's pale blue satin wedding gown. It had been carefully wrapped and kept in the large blanket chest for many years. Her mother had died two years after Hannah was born. She dimly remembered a dark-haired woman singing to her at bedtime.

Tears welled up in Hannah's eyes. "If only she had lived. I have missed havin' me mother. To be sure, it's her face I'd like to see smilin' up at me on this holy day."

Somehow just touching the gown made Hannah feel connected to the mother gone for so many years.

Indian Will walked Hannah down the aisle. He was dressed in soft deerskin leggings and shirt decorated with intricate patterns of quills and beads. His long, graying braids were carefully crisscrossed with rawhide strips and turkey feathers. He could feel his heart swelling. It was an honor to be a part of this peculiar white man's ritual.

There was Seamus, waiting at the altar, his knees of jelly and his heart flip-flopping about. He was handsomely attired in a dark suit and tweed vest. His grin reached from ear to ear.

Hannah walked toward him, her arm linked to Will's. Her dark brown hair tumbled down past her shoulders. On her head was a delicate wreath of pink wild mountain roses that matched the ones she carried in her right hand. The dark of her hair and eyes contrasted with the light blue satin gown and the pink flowers. She was startlingly beautiful.

For a moment Seamus couldn't breathe. "'Tis the love that has filled me so full, there be no room in me lungs." For a moment he feared that he might faint.

They left St. Patrick's Church at a fast clip. The old buckboard lurched and bumped along the ruts. Indian Will in his *kastoweh*, feathers flying every which way, guided the mule. The newly married couple held on to each other as much for safety as for passion. It was a curious sight to those they passed on the road.

They traveled through the gap in Knobly Mountain, passed by the village of Frankfort, galloped over Patterson Creek Mountain, and crossed the South Branch of the Potomac into the village of Romney, Virginia.

The Reverend John MacIntyre remembered Seamus from the funeral and was pleased that the couple wanted to be married. It wasn't good for a woman to be alone. She was fortunate to find such a handsome, strong Presbyterian. The good reverend understood why Indian Will walked her down the aisle. After all, he had been a friend of the family for two generations.

Indian Will believed these back-to-back weddings were strong medicine, very strong medicine indeed.

Granny Sare

She was colorful, from her rich chocolate skin to the woolen shawl, the yarns of which were earthen hues of burnished orange, yellow, green, and brown. With a twined hemp rope, she led a tall-legged, horned wether named Jacob. Slung over the back of the sheep were baskets of all shapes filled with skeins of wool. Some baskets were filled with natural yarns of white, black, gray, while others contained plant-dyed skeins matching the colors in her shawl.

Stopping under a black walnut tree, the woman filled a large basketful of fallen green-hulled nuts and then continued toward the village of Frankfort. In her left hand was a small, many-pronged branch covered with billowing white fleece. In her right hand she twirled a spindle, and as it dropped toward the ground, a growing thread appeared. When the spindle reached the ground, she wound the thread around the shaft. Her hand would reach toward the fleece and the process would begin again.

She came to barter her baskets and colorful yarns for woven goods, mainly blankets. Her name was Sarah. People in the village thought the Old Testament name suited her. After all, she was elderly with tight-curled graying hair, and she held many a newborn in her generous arms.

The settlers sought her not only because she had the best baskets and yarns, but because she had presided over the birth of their children and now their children's children. Sarah was the best midwife to be found in these remote mountains. People were beholden to her.

Perhaps it began out of lazy speech, but growingly, it was out of fondness. Most people referred to her as Granny Sare.

No one was sure where she came from. Some thought she might have been a runaway slave. But if so, that had happened way before their time. At first the speculators, who came through the area looking to buy slaves or catch the ones that had escaped, didn't pay much attention to Granny Sare. She was so old that she wasn't worth a plug of tobacco in the Richmond slave markets.

It was a bad time for slaves in Appalachia—not that they ever had it good. Cotton-growing boomed in the South, and the need for more slaves grew. The owners of small plantations in the mountains began to regard slaves more and more as a marketable commodity much like cattle and hogs. Children were sold off at puberty. When a husband and wife were sold, they were often separated. Even if a family were kept together, it was still a common practice to lease black males to distant plantations. Often the slaves were allowed only a short visit at Christmas.

Children were taught to hide when the speculators came. It was known that the speculators would kidnap little children, grabbing them away, right in front of their mothers.

These days, it was not unusual to see wagons heading south, black males chained together like convicts, women and small children walking behind. A traveler passing through the village reported counting as many as three hundred slaves in one caravan down by the Shenandoah River.

For most runaway slaves, it was not enough to pass over the Mason-Dixon Line into Pennsylvania. It was Canaan Land—Canada—that offered freedom with the lesser risk of being captured.

Granny Sare lived out by Patterson Creek, way up in the hills. There were stories about her living in a basket. They were partially right. Her dwelling was of wattle and daub and looked like an inverted basket with a lid of corrugated tin to keep the rain out.

Wattle and daub was an ancient method of building. The first Colonial settlers of Jamestown made their dwellings in that manner. Upright posts were set in the ground and green saplings were woven into walls between them. The walls were then plastered with a mixture of river clay, grasses, and dung.

Next to Granny's house was an open-sided shelter, an outdoor kitchen, for cooking and dye pots. Granny Sare emptied baskets of green-hulled walnuts into a large iron pot to soak.

"Dey'll make me some purty deep brown color," she muttered.

From the rafters hung bunches of wild coreopsis, Queen Anne's lace, and sumac. On the ground lay piles of lichen. These also would be used to make the colors of her yarns.

In a far corner was a tin bucket that she used for soaking yarn in a mordant. Some plant dyes needed help in adhering to the wool. A mordant of alum, chrome, or even urine might be used. Granny Sare believed the strongest men produced the strongest mordant.

She had seen the muscular, copper-haired Irishman. "Dat man, if he'd jist conterbute to de pot, de dye would stick real good."

She'd give it some thought. Think how best to ask him.

High on a knoll was a clearing where her eighteen sheep grazed during the day. Each evening she would bring the sheep down to the safety of shelter a hundred feet from her dwelling. A large rock jutted out from the hillside, forming a roof to a shallow cave. Her wattle fence secured the area in front with just enough room for the sheep, the manger, and a water bucket. Outside the gate was tethered a hybrid dog, more wolf than anything else. Granny Sare called him Goliath.

It wasn't obvious to the eye, but another large boulder in the far back of the compound, on the right side, obscured a small niche. The only way into it was to scramble up and over the top. It was too difficult for the sheep to manage.

Granny Sare sighed with relief. "Dey'll ne'er find de secret."

The Linden Tree

By late summer, almost a year had passed since the day of the double wedding. The giddiness of new love hadn't worn off, but there was a growing depth to their relationship that came with familiarity. A stroke on the cheek, a nuzzle on the nape of the neck, just simple touching was all that was needed. A strong feeling of connection permeated their lives.

Seamus was passionate in words and deeds. There was little middle ground for him. He had strong opinions about most everything. That was not all bad since Hannah and he agreed on a lot.

But there were those times when they banged heads, and Seamus knew he had an equal adversary. In particular, it was Hannah's enterprising nature that got to him. Hannah had made coverlets on the old barn loom since she was twelve. Over the years she had become quite skilled. Granny Sare was her main supplier of yarn.

All this made Seamus proud, until she set up shop on Wednesdays at the Stone Hotel. Hannah wanted new chairs for around the table, and she hoped to sell or barter enough coverlets to get them. The wages that Seamus brought home from the Railroad Company weren't enough for luxury items, so this would be one way of doing it.

Seamus tried his persuasion. "There be rough men who stop at the hotel. 'Tisn't safe. What'll people think of me wife needin' to work in such a place? Surely it'll be better if I sell them at the market."

Well, he tried, but Hannah smiled widely and said, "I have done this before. I set up shop before my father was taken sick. I know how to handle rough men. Look at yerself. Why do ya care about what other people think? I will only do sellin' when ya are away. I'm not about to take precious time away from our bein' together."

Seamus was getting nowhere and when he felt the blood rising to his face, he turned and went outside. He was trying to keep his temper under control.

Maybe it was just the weather that made him irritable. It was hot and humid and reminded him of the Paw Paw Tunnel, of the day when the twisted ankle and snake intertwined, searing into his psyche. Hot, humid, barely breathable air, and pain wrapped neatly as one. Even with the years passing, days like this sent mild shocks of constriction around his heart.

He need not make things worse and blow up at Hannah.

"'Tis not good fer me temper to get me mouth runnin'. 'Tis the love we share that matters, not the winnin' of the argument."

He looked up and saw her coming toward him. When she had settled next to him, he decided it was just fine to close his eyes and breathe away his fears.

Hannah hated humid days. The slightest movement sent sweat down her forehead, stinging, salty rivulets channeling into her eyes. Her hair frantically frizzed in opposing directions adding to her distress. She was thankful that Seamus stopped the argument. She closed her eyes and dreamed of winter, dancing on new-fallen snow in her blue-flowered shift.

The ancient linden tree cast its shade across the lawn as late afternoon approached. Under its large, heart-shaped leaves were winged seed pods. For a while, only the sound of worker bees could be heard; then came absolute silence. Nature seemed to be holding her breath. A slight whisper of a breeze began to flutter the leaves. Hannah and Seamus sighed with relief when the wind grew stronger and began to blow in storm clouds. Though they didn't speak of it, both knew they would stay immovable until the rain soaked them into coolness.

What they didn't realize was what the old linden tree was about to do. The fluttering leaves began to lift as the growing force of the wind turned branches into undulating, churning arms. Cross winds fingered the underside of the leaves, exposing their gossamer, fairy-winged seeds. The whirling wind and dark, moody clouds set the stage as the great linden gave a tremendous orgasmic shudder and hurled countless thousands of winged pods into the air.

Hannah and Seamus laughed uncontrollably. "Come, let's see how many we can catch," challenged Hannah.

They raced to the grass, catching seeds by the handfuls as the cooling drops of rain fell.

It was a spell that the tree cast. The couple, soaked and blanketed with pods, lay on the ground and shuddered their own seed together.

The Famine Irish

He called them all "Paddy." Eckhart wasn't about to learn their real names. They were all unpronounceable as far as he was concerned.

Seamus winced. "'Tis the same agin. It be like we were treated at the Paw Paw Tunnel. 'Tis a promise I give meself. 'Tis the Gaelic name I'll use."

Eckhart had put Seamus in charge of the Irish, knowing he could speak their strange language. Seamus was determined to honor each of them by using their Christian Gaelic names.

The German workers, Eckhart understood. He could understand the dialect.

There was something peculiar about these new Irish immigrants, setting them apart from the earlier laborers Eckhart had hired. They were a different breed. It seemed to the burly foreman that their faces partially masked a depth of despair he had never seen before. Eckhart didn't want to get too close. He had enough difficulty getting the tracks laid alongside the Potomac to Cumberland.

Seamus sensed the difference too. These recent Irish were even poorer, seemed beaten down by all of life itself.

"'Tis as if the stuff that makes them who they are has been kicked out. 'Tis hard to imagine."

Seamus listened to their stories. Since Seamus had left Ireland, matters had gone from bad to terribly wrong. Young Fergus was the first to speak.

"Did ya know now that most all the land in Ireland is owned by the English and the Protestant Irish? 'Tis the Catholics who are not allowed to own the land. Allowed we are to rent wee parcels and build dwellings, but the cussed landowners can kick us off the land on a mere whim. There be no security. The homes we build have mud sides and dirt floors, sometimes no chimneys, no windows. What be the sense to build a grander dwelling? It would be all the more quickly taken away. 'Tis true that large families share their space, sleepin' on straw with their chickens and pigs. 'Tis fortunate we are to have a roof over our heads."

Then Donal spoke. "'Tis the potato that provides our food. 'Tis often the only crop. We be callin' the months of July and August the hungry times. The old potato crop, 'tis gone or rotten. 'Tis too early fer the new harvest. There be many beggars. Would ya believe now that many made to beg are the direct descendants of the great Irish High Kings?"

Seamus felt a wrenching sadness for his Ireland, for these men. How could so many go through so much, come so far, and end up with so little? It could not be worse.

Compassion

Seamus began to understand. When anger and frustration gave way to drunken fights, he knew it was their way of release from their tragic lives. He had done the same in his past at the Paw Paw. But now he was determined to change that predictable behavior.

"No doubt I can pound some heads with the best of them, but 'tis the respect I be needin'."

Gradually, disputes were defused by Seamus and his golden, persuasive tongue. Often he would turn anger into humor, challenges into competitive games. He initiated contests of spike driving and tossing railroad ties to channel their frustrations in less damaging ways.

Seamus thought, *'Tis better sense than black eyes and bloody noses*. Rarely was there a man whom Seamus couldn't turn around.

However, there was one. A man whose name really was Paddy, or so he claimed. He stuck like a blackthorn in Seamus' side. Nothing went unchallenged.

Seamus muttered to himself, "If I say good mornin', Paddy points out how buggy and humid it is. If I ask him to help clear the way for tracks, he argues which direction they should go. A grand annoyance, he is."

"Hey, Paddy, if ya go any slower, ya'll meet yer arse on the way back," goaded Seamus.

The hard fact was, when Paddy got down to work, he was the very best. This so irritated Seamus that he lost his temper more than was good for his status as leader. He recognized a familiar hardheadedness in this man. It was a kind of "takes one to know one" situation.

It was at a point when the fuming Seamus and the smirking Paddy were doing their best to one-up the other that Eckhart again brought out the one-hundred-pound maul.

Seamus remembered well the humiliation and exhaustion he had felt. "Dear Blessed Mother," he fervently prayed, "'tis not fer me. All the angels no can help lift that maul."

He felt great relief when the task was given to Paddy. The results were as they should have been. He almost slammed the damn maul on his foot several times. The bend in the rail stubbornly remained even when he managed to hit it.

After Eckhart demonstrated how the maul could properly be used, he turned to the two men and said, "You both have been squabbling like little children. If ya can't straighten it out between yourselves, perhaps I'll have to help. You'll be dealin' with me, and it won't be pleasant."

Paddy got the point, and so did Seamus. Matters began to turn around for the two rivals after Seamus fessed up. He told Paddy, he too had been given the maul. "'Tis no better I did than ya."

Later that evening, Eckhart invited Seamus to his private campfire. It was only by invitation that anyone went near the boss after work had stopped. Seamus hunkered down, then lowered himself to the ground, sitting splay-legged in front of the fire.

Eckhart said, "I like to give credit to people when it is due. Despite your problem with Paddy, you're doin' well with the Irish, keeping the peace and gettin' the work done. I appreciate it. No doubt you and Paddy will straighten matters out. There's an old sayin' that 'work praises the man.'" Seamus felt embarrassed over the compliment, but what followed eased the awkwardness.

"There's another piece of credit that is also due. My hundred-pound maul has a name. It is called the John Davis. It's named after a Welshman who works at the Mount Savage Brickyards. I stole the idea from him. To my knowledge we are the only two people around here who can lift that maul properly. I'd kindly appreciate if you'd keep that private, just between you and me. Understand that some of man's best ideas can come from other people. Be open to that as you work with your crew."

Seamus became steadily closer to the men he supervised. As a team they bent their backs and muscles into creating a remarkable railroad. Those tracks would follow the flowing Potomac to Cumberland, climb Backbone Mountain to the Cheat River Valley, travel along the Tygert River, and God willing, make it to Wheeling.

The summer day was hot. The locusts buzzed their mating call from the tall grass. The smell of tarred ties and acrid human sweat mingled with the sounds of breaking rock. The rock used as ballast for the tracks was tamped in place to make a solid base for the ties and rails.

The laborers leaned on long bars, throwing their weight in a circular motion. Seeing thirty men settling ballast in such a way was like viewing a rhythmic dance. After the ties were laid in place, men would straddle a long section of rail and carry it into position. It was easiest to walk the rail, starting with the same foot in cadence. In doing so the men looked as if they waddled like ganders. Spiking the rails to the ties had its own music. The more rhythmically the laborers swung their malls, the faster the job was completed.

To set the pace and lessen the monotony, work songs were invented on the spot.

"Work all day...huh, Sugar in my tay...huh, Not much pay...huh, Whiskey at night...huh, Get into a fight...huh, Not too bright...huh." And so it would continue long into the day, each laborer, in turn, adding his own phrase.

The men who did the tamping of ballast, the carrying of rails, and the setting of spikes were first nicknamed "ganders." Seamus and his crew preferred to call them "gandy dancers." It seemed lighthearted, more descriptive. Eventually each man, in his own turn, would dance the dance.

The tracks were getting close to the wagon trail that followed Dan's Run. The road bent sharply to the left and traveled to the ford at Patterson Creek. The tracks would follow alongside the road, sandwiched between it and the river before crossing over the Potomac, heading toward Cumberland.

Seamus liked this stretch of tracks, as Broad Hollow wasn't far, and he could spend the evenings at home with Hannah. He was looking forward to the time Hannah and he could sit on their porch and listen to the trains rumble down the tracks.

That pleasant daydream was broken when one of his men urgently yelled for him to come to the head of the work line. Seamus had a sinking feeling. Two tarriers blasting rock for the track's gravel beds had instead blown themselves up. Another man lay severely bleeding after being hit by a flying shard.

Seamus paled at the sight and began to tremble. "None of the saints in heaven can stop this from happenin'. Is there no mercy or protection fer this miserable lot?" The horror of Connor's death struck him yet again.

It was Eckart's way. He'd stockpile the bodies of deceased workers on a covered buckboard at the far back end of the line until there were enough to take time to bury.

"Might just as well do a bunch all at once than one here and then one there," he would comment.

Cholera continued to follow the workers just as it had at the canal tunnel. In some ways it was worse now. There was no hospital or Doc Adams or Purslane Cemetery. Nonetheless, Seamus insisted that each man deserved a proper burial.

Fears ran high when someone died of disease. No one wanted to go near the body, as the contagion could spread rapidly. Some crews would just leave the body behind.

Seamus held out a fistful of straws. "'Tis the fairest way. Who draws the shortest one is to stuff the body into a feed sack and place it on the last wagon. Then it not be fer ya to do agin 'til all the crew has had a turn."

By the end of this day, the buckboard would carry seven dead men. The heat of summer had begun to putrify the bodies. So at the sharp turn of Dan's Run road, Seamus was sent to find a burial ground.

Seamus was familiar with the land. It wasn't far from his parents' farm, and he had hunted deer close by. He remembered the bluff where he had shot a fine eleven-point buck. After gutting it, he had paused a moment to take in the view. The river could be seen in the distance. There was something special about that place. Now he knew it would become more so.

Four men cut a path up the hill for the buckboard to follow, while seven men dug seven graves. They must have thought that this would be their ending as well. Five of the dead men were Irish and two were German. No one knew their relatives. Surely they had families. Now they would disappear forever into the earth, graves marked only by small river rocks. The men had fled from poverty, danger, and sickness, only to die precisely that way.

Buried high on the bluff, their graves overlooked the tracks they had helped build, tracks that had led them to their graves. They would vanish into the earth, buried without coffins, dressed only in the clothes they had on, never to be properly mourned by those who had loved them. These were the nameless men, joining a long procession of thousands who had gone before and who would soon follow.

Seamus had remembered Irish stories of how the ancient Druids believed oak groves were sacred. He had the graves placed near twin oaks. Several yards away a massive, sweeping oak stood as if keeping guard. Seamus knew the decaying bodies would provide nourishment for the trees' seeking roots.

He stood somberly in the fading light and thought to himself, *'Tis the men's souls that'll merge with the oaks' lifeblood and make holy the grove.*

The Celebration
November 5, 1842

Indian Will harnessed Hannah's old mule to the buckboard. The animal was fondly called Whiplash, because he often stopped abruptly in the middle of a fast trot just to look around or swipe a mouthful of grass. This action often sent the driver and passengers onto the mule's backside. At that point the beast earned names less fond.

Whiplash was unpredictable and downright cussed. Seamus, when he drove the wagon, was just about as stubborn and ill behaved as that animal. The unpredictable was predictable. Whiplash had a mind of his own, which was not often in compliance with Seamus. Sometimes he just stopped for no apparent reason. Seamus swore, "Ya bleedin' mule." He pulled, and pushed, while the mule loudly brayed and dug his hooves into the earth. They were equals in the struggle.

Hannah would untangle herself from the harness and hand Seamus the reins. She had told him, "Seamus, I know ye're brighter than the mule. Pay attention to me. I'll show ya what 'tis ya need to do."

She'd scratch Whiplash's long ears, speak lovingly, and hold a carrot a short distance from his nose. She had learned years ago never to travel with Whiplash without taking along carrots. Soon the mule, munching his carrot, would continue contentedly down the road.

Today Indian Will was to drive the mule. He never had problems with Whiplash. He could tell by the curious twitching of his ears what Whiplash was about to do. Snapping the whip lightly on the animal's hindquarters, he'd growl unintelligible sounds, and Whiplash would proceed smoothly onward.

It was going to be a day like no other. It was November 5, 1842, and the railroad tracks had been completed to Cumberland. There was to be a big celebration as the first train arrived.

Will had seen a train once from a great distance. He wasn't sure he liked it. There were many people who didn't like the railroad and for about as many reasons.

Stories were told about how a cow had been hit and killed by a train. Better yet, how a bull had stood his ground in the middle of the tracks only to be sent tumbling down a thirty-foot bank by a fast-moving engine. Fortunately, the bull survived. But trains seemed to endanger valuable livestock.

There were also concerns about the profitable stagecoaches. The National Road, coming out of Baltimore, through Cumberland, heading on to Ohio, was the best in the land. What need was there for more expense?

Some favored the canal system as the safest and best way to ship goods. While it had yet to reach Cumberland, at least canals had been around longer.

Others just didn't like newfangled inventions and, for that matter, change of any sort.

"Hannah, darlin', today, 'tis a grand day. Next to the weddin', 'tis the best day in me life. Jist think, the railroad is the finest invention in all of history and 'twill be us who see it arrive at the station. 'Tis'll be the grandest way to travel. 'Tis the world that'll be changed fer sure." He thought quietly to himself, *'Tis anything better than this stubborn old mule.*

After all the difficult work and the men who had died laying down track, it was inconceivable to him that it wouldn't prove to be the most profitable and the best form of transportation.

"Aye, Seamus, but truthfully 'tis a coach and four pulled by a matching pair of grays that I dream of ridin' in. No machine in all the world could be so beautiful. 'Tis also the ladies and their fancy hats I'll be wantin' to see. Oh, Seamus, would ya please take me to the large hotel so I can sip a fine glass of Madeira wine?"

Hannah was just plain excited to see something new and to be in the middle of all the commotion.

There was a moment of silence.

Realizing her ommission, Hannah added, "Oh, 'tis also the train I would like to see. It's jist the whole idea of a metal contraption pullin' a long line of coaches seems a bit peculiar."

The town of Cumberland was crowded with stagecoaches, Conestoga wagons, buckboards of all sizes. People were pushing, shoving, and running to get the best position for the best view when the train arrived. Indian Will tied the mule and buckboard to a hitch behind the Columbian Inn on South Street.

As they walked up the hill toward the terminus, people stared at Will. Seamus thought that he looked more than ever weathered and venerable but assumed that it was the amazing hat topped with turkey feathers that caught everyone's eye.

But it wasn't the hat. Will knew better. There hadn't been many Indians in the area for a long while. Accounts of raiding Shawnees, massacres, and whites being burned at the stake lived on vividly in people's memories. It was less than a hundred years ago when the French and Indian War had occurred. People didn't forget, and mistrust of Indians was still prevalent.

President Andrew Jackson had signed the Indian Removal Act in 1830. By 1839, fourteen thousand Cherokee were marched through Tennessee, Kentucky, Missouri, and on to the Arkansas Indian Territory. Four thousand died along the way from hunger, disease, and exposure.

"*Nunna daul tsuny*" meant "trail where they cried."

It's not just white people who don't forget, who have reason to mistrust, thought Will.

He had recently seen twenty black slaves chained together, being marched toward the Richmond auction houses. Those people also had their own trail of tears. A great sadness came over the Indian as he stood silently among the laughing, jostling, expectant crowd.

The air began to vibrate, and people grew quiet. Toward the terminus approached an amazing sight. It resembled a giant grasshopper with iron legs. Steam belched from a tall pipe in front as an excruciatingly loud, gasping, chugging sound filled the air. Hannah and Will backed away from the tracks in appalled horror. Some clapped and hooted and crowded closer. Proudly Seamus stood close to the iron beast. If he could be an inanimate object, he'd choose to be this.

As the November afternoon air began to turn cold, Hannah finally convinced Seamus to leave the terminus. When they arrived at the Columbian Inn, Hannah insisted that they go inside. Indian Will already knew why. He also knew that whiskey brought out a side of him that was dangerous. Will said he'd wait with Whiplash. Give the mule some grain and water before the trip home.

"Hannah, darlin', why do we need to go into a tavern?"

"Because, Seamus, 'tis the Madeira wine I would like. We need to celebrate."

Ah, thought Seamus, *she really liked the blessed train after all.*

Hannah chose a settle off to the side where the warming fire crackled. Seamus ordered her Madeira and himself a whiskey and then began to talk excitedly about the mechanics of the engine.

Hannah, with her glass raised, put her fingers gently on his lips. "A toast, my dear Seamus." And before she could continue, he said, "To the railroad!"

They drank to that and Hannah again raised her glass. "A toast, dear Seamus."

"To what else, dear Hannah?"

"To our baby inside me," said she.

Seamus dropped his glass, spilled her Madeira, picked her up, and twirled her around. It was Hannah who turned blushing red when Seamus announced the event for all to hear.

Sitting down, he ordered yet another whiskey and topped off the wine glass.

"When, Hannah, darlin'?"

"May," she whispered.

Pickles

Hannah grew extremely fond of salt-brined pickles, not the kind she made, only the special ones found at Ratcliff's Market in Frankfort. Seamus did his best to keep her supplied.

When Granny Sare came to the cabin to barter her supplies of yarn and baskets for woven blankets, Hannah was excited to tell her about the coming baby. "Granny, would ya please help me? Be my midwife?" The old woman's eyes clouded, and she seemed to hide behind her face.

"Sweet chil', I'd love to be with ye, but dese days, I'm 'bout another part of de Lord's work. It takes me away. I ain't able to make de promise."

For Hannah, Granny's answer came as an unexpected shock. She didn't want to give birth alone. She was scared and had always thought Granny Sare would be there with her. Granny had helped her mother, been there when she was born.

The look of abandonment and despair in Hannah's eyes made Granny's heart melt. She felt so stretched and torn these days. It was difficult being needed in so many life giving ways.

How could she promise when she never knew when the others would need her?

Tears slid down Hannah's face. These days she was emotional, crying over burnt johnnycakes or the moon glistening off the rocks in her garden, and now Granny's refusal to promise. She missed having a mother, missed the security of knowing what would happen.

"Sweet Hannah chil', ye have time yet to go. Send Seamus when ye feel the kicking inside yer belly. Maybe den I can say for sur'. He's goin' be a fine one, don't ye worry."

Hannah hadn't felt strongly which it would be. Now it seemed likely that Granny Sare knew. Seamus had agreed to choose the boy's name and Hannah, just in case, would choose the girl's.

It cut deeply inside Seamus that his parents refused to acknowledge his marriage to Hannah.

"She is Protestant," they cried, as if he hadn't already said that. It seemed more upsetting to them than Connor's death.

Clearly, marriage was chosen and the death was not. In their minds that's what made the difference.

"Catholics and Protestants don't mix. They're like a fox in a chicken house," his parents insisted.

He felt that he had let them down in so many ways. If only they had responded in some small compassionate way. Hannah and he could use some loving support.

As the days and months slipped by, Hannah overcame morning sickness and her belly grew. It became so round, her lap seemed to disappear. She could no longer play her dulcimer.

Seamus cleaned and refinished the Canady family cradle, while Hannah wove a small coverlet out of delicate, soft gray and white yarns. The pattern was called Bethlehem Star. When she began to feel alone or sorry for herself, she would think of young Mary giving birth in a stable. God willing, Hannah would be in her walnut poster bed, surrounded by her mother's old quilts.

Seamus did his very best to keep Hannah's spirits up. He told her every day that she was beautiful.

"I even love ya more than whiskey," he'd say.

He would tease her when she descended into dark moods. But never did he share his amazement as he watched her thin waist disappear, her gracious walk turn into a waddle. He knew that would be dangerous. Still, without a doubt, to Seamus, there was no one more beautiful.

As the months passed, the baby began to roll and tumble inside Hannah, punching with such strength that it alarmed Seamus. He went to fetch Granny Sare. Her eyes widened when she saw Hannah.

"Darlin' chil', ye're goin' to give birth to a young'n the size of dat man of yers. What ye been eat'n?"

Granny felt Hannah's belly, felt the kicking turmoil inside, and determined mid-May was the time this child would choose to be born. She sensed that she just might be needed during this birth. Hannah was a small woman, and this baby would be big.

She explained in great detail what she would need for the birthing, what the signs would be, how to count the birth pains, and when to send for her. Under no circumstances should he leave Hannah alone.

This produced a dilemma for Seamus. Should Indian Will fetch Granny Sare or should he go himself? Will had more knowledge and knew about medicines. Seamus might miss the birth altogether if he went.

Hannah was clear. "'Tis our baby, Seamus. I need ya to be with me."

The rain fell on the shake roof with such a force that it produced a thudding din inside the cabin. At first Hannah thought there must have been a leak in the roof, because the chair she was sitting on was wet. The shocking realization that the water had come from her own body, that her birth water had broken, sent her into a trembling, frightened state. Her emotions swirled around so fast that Hannah felt faint. She called for Seamus. Seamus went to find Will. Will went to find Granny Sare.

As Hannah lay on the bed, the labor pains increased with decided intensity. Seamus made sure there was hot water and plenty of clean cloths. As the contractions surged, he'd hold Hannah's forehead and tell her how much he loved her. In between the pains, he told her how pleased he was to name their son after his brother, Connor.

She smiled at Seamus and said, "Jist in case it's a girl, her name will be Mairéad."

It was Irish for the name Mary, and in this particular pregnancy, Hannah felt very close to the holy woman. She also had no mother to comfort her. She was frightened.

Time has its way. It can fly by so fast, you wonder what happened. Other times it just crawls along. For the two, time seemed to fly and creep all at once.

When Granny Sare arrived, she was drenched from the storm. Hannah's contractions were so strong, they lifted her halfway down the bed. The baby's head had crowned and within minutes, out slid a red-faced baby with copper-colored hair. The squalling cry announced a healthy baby's arrival. It was a girl.

"Sweet, lovely Mairéad," Seamus repeated over and over as he held their tiny child.

If ever there had been preference of boy over girl, it disappeared. Mairéad already had her father's heart twined securely around her small, delicate finger.

Granny Sare beamed and turned her attention back to Hannah. She suddenly grew somber as she sensed that something wasn't as it should be. Granny often experienced this situation at lambing time. There was a second baby attempting to be born. It was in trouble. Hannah's contractions were growing weaker.

Granny carefully felt around the birth canal and slowly pulled on the baby's head.

"Hannah, chil', push for all ye're worth. Now. Agin. Now!"

Gradually there emerged a dark-haired baby. Instead of healthy rose-colored skin, its face was blue. The umbilical cord was wrapped around its neck, and there was no sign of breathing.

Granny quickly released the cord from the baby's neck, firmly picked the infant up by its feet, and swung it three times around, head over heels. Then she sucked the mucus from its mouth and a small, weak wail emerged.

To everyone's stunned amazement, baby boy Connor had made his way into the world.

Kindred

Deirdre and Padraig Malone looked awkward and tense as the front door opened to the cabin. Seamus and Hannah, with anxious trepidation, welcomed his parents to their home.

Seamus had done all the sweet-talking to his parents, persuading them to come. "They're yer only grandchildren. They're darlin'. The blessed Mother of Jesus wouldn't want ya to miss bein' part of their lives. After all they've done nothin' to ya. They're sweet babes need'n their grandparents." He wore them down a bit. Grudgingly they agreed to come.

Deidre still held on to her anger. "Why had Seamus married such a heathen?" Protestants in Ireland had murdered her brother and now their blood mingled in her grandchildren's veins. She could not hide her disapproval. Hannah felt it like an icy cold shawl laid upon her shoulders.

Seamus was visibly nervous. After all, it was the first time all four of them had been in the same room together. His father didn't help matters either by standing rigidly with his eyes carefully studying the plank flooring.

Hannah felt herself slipping downward into her own self-righteous indignation. Then Seamus gently squeezed her hand. In a flicker of a candle, she pulled herself away from that emotional quagmire and flashed at the elder Malones a lovingly warm, devastating smile. She took Deirdre's hand in hers and gently led the woman toward the comfortable settle.

Infants and their parents' dreams for them often create opportunities to bring estranged families together. The new unblemished lives and guileless innocence stand in judgment of the pettiness and sins collected as people age.

Hannah couldn't bring her parents back from the grave, but perhaps she could win a piece of his parents' hearts for Seamus. Seamus had grieved over their anger and refusal to acknowledge Hannah as his wife. After all, it was not easy for Hannah to open her heart to them, but she was determined. It was Hannah who had sent Seamus to the Malone homestead with the invitation.

Deirdre Malone pursed her lips and looked around the cabin critically. "'Tisn't much to find wrong here. 'Tis as clean and neat as a proper Irish home."

The woven coverlet folded over the back of the settle colored with yarns of indigo and rose madder even sent a tinge of envy through the elder woman.

But it was when Hannah returned with the two swaddled infants that those thin, set lips began to twitch into a smile.

Padraig Malone finally unglued his eyes from the plank floor, and as he looked upon the sleeping babies, reluctant tears flowed down his cheeks.

How very proud Seamus and Hannah were to introduce Mairéad and Connor to their only living grandparents.

"Of course they must be baptized soon," stated Deidre Malone, "and raised Catholic."

Hannah subtly dug her nails into Seamus' palm as they stood side by side holding hands. Seamus nodded and Hannah forced her face into the warmest smile possible. They were prepared. They had known it would be expected.

Mrs. Malone sighed in relief. "At least the infants won't be raised as heathens," she stated.

How could she continue to see Hannah as the enemy when she seemed so agreeable? After all, it was Catholic blood that flowed through the infants' veins as well. Surely Catholic blood was stronger than Protestant.

Padraig Malone sat holding the two infants, staring into their faces, and said not a word.

Both families had christening gowns, so it was decided that Mairéad would wear the smocked one that Hannah had worn. Connor would wear the Malone Irish lace. Hannah thought it would look better the other way around but again wisely decided that some battles need not be won.

The following day, Hannah and Seamus carried the twins, with Indian Will behind, down the path to the moss-covered banks of the creek. A soft breeze fluttered the nearby ferns as the sunlight through the trees dappled the ground. Gently kneeling beside the stream, Seamus and Hannah cupped the cool water in their hands, trickling it over the foreheads of Mairéad and Connor.

Together they said, "I baptize thee in the name of the Father, Son, and Holy Ghost."

Indian Will knew this would be the continuation of more double medicine.

Deirdre had already sent a message to Father McCauley to prepare a baptism for two on Sunday morning.

Separation

After the Baltimore and Ohio Railroad reached Cumberland and the celebrations subsided, the push westward to the Ohio River came to a grinding stop. The Virginia legislature rescinded permission for the tracks to continue to Parkersburg. Instead they were to continue to Wheeling.

That single change in direction presented difficulties with the terrain that seemed insurmountable. These were further complicated by the fact that Pennsylvania refused to have any tracks from Virginia placed on its soil. Routing the tracks to Pittsburgh would have made a lot of sense; however, because of northern competition and perhaps jealousy, permission was not granted. Money was short, and taking the tracks to Wheeling would be extremely difficult. Arguments ensued and tempers flared.

For six years it seemed that the Ohio part of the B&O Railroad would never happen. Arguments and delays continued, but on another front, significant progress was being made.

Near the settlement of Mount Savage, good deposits of iron ore, coal, and fire clay were discovered. That made it possible, in Western Maryland, to manufacture iron products needed by the railroads and the canal.

Two fifty-foot-high iron furnaces were in operation throughout the day and night. The Railroad Company also built a rolling mill. Within a year it produced iron rail, the first to be manufactured in the United States. Previously, all rail had been imported from Britain. It was yet another step of independence from the mother country, and the immigrant Irish especially took delight in that.

It was Eckhart who sent the letter to Seamus. "I need ya agin' as foreman. Mount Savage has burgeoned, growin' up to perhaps two thousand people. Many are Irish and German immigrants hired as iron workers. Of course I've hired some for layin' down a short line of track from Mount Savage to Cumberland. Ya did so well by me in the past, can ya lend me a hand?"

Seamus was flattered to be asked by Eckhart. It stroked his ego. He admired the man, and working on the tracks seemed to be in his blood. When he heard the train traveling along the Potomac not far from their cabin, he felt consumed with longing. Next to Hannah and the twins, the train was the love of his life.

He sat by the hog pen looking out on the field of corn he had planted, and rationalized, "Just for one year."

He'd make more money. After all, he needed to think about the twins. Hannah deserved good things. The twins were two years old, and Hannah didn't seem to need a lot of help. He didn't like farming all that much. He'd be home for Christmas, which would break up the year. He'd promise this would be the last time. He had already convinced himself. Now he needed to convince Hannah.

It wasn't that easy.

"But what about the nights," she said, "when we fit ourselves together like two spoons and yer arms wrap me in yer embrace? Now, won't ya be missin' that?"

"Oh, Hannah, 'tis not fair," he responded. "God and the saints know I will. 'Tis the money. It'll put us a bit ahead. Sure ya know I'm not much of a farmer. What Eckhart offers me, 'tis what I do best. 'Tis the only job I've done well. Christmas, I'll be off fer a bit. 'Tis only a few months from now. I'll be back then. The work ends in the spring. I promise, 'tis then finished fer me."

He reached for her. Pulled her close until their bodies pressed tightly together. They each could feel the other's heartbeat strongly as they held each other. Tears slid down their faces and for a fleeting moment, Seamus was unsure.

The following week, Hannah stood on the cabin steps and bravely bade him a safe journey. They kissed long and gently. Then she pressed his hand to her cheek. Seamus hesitated, kissed Mairéad and Connor, and turned to Hannah one last time.

"Hannah, darlin', I'll be back by Christmas. 'Tis a promise." He forced himself to leave quickly.

Why do I have these naggin' feelings of guilt? 'Tis hard on me too. I'm doin' it fer the family, aren't I?

Mount Savage was crowded with people. Men were shouting in different languages that blended into one unintelligible babble. The night sky was lit orange, obliterating the stars from view. There was power in the burning smells and blasting furnaces. The intensity of the place crackled with danger.

Seamus watched the puddlers stir the molten iron with long poles while others skimmed off the impurities. The heat seemed unbearable to him, so he kept back. Seamus had heard stories of the workers losing their balance and slipping into the fiery cauldrons, a death that, despite the heat, sent shivers down his back.

He knew in a visceral way that the tracks would yet again be made from the lifeblood of immigrants. Sinew, flesh, and bone would merge with the iron of the rails.

The months passed by slowly for Hannah. Sometimes it seemed as if time itself had stopped. When the twins came teetering through the room or found a new word to utter, she would regret their fast growing, regret the fast passing of time, regret how much Seamus was missing.

The snow came early in December and didn't stop. Day after day it fell gently from the sky. Hannah made many trips to the wood pile, stacking as many logs inside the cabin as possible. Then she trudged through the mounting snow to the root cellar, dug away from the door, and carried the root vegetables on an old sledge to the cool pantry. The smokehouse was next. Its contents also were emptied. She made sure that Whiplash had access to plenty of hay. She put the water in among the straw hoping it wouldn't freeze.

Perhaps I'm foolish, thought Hannah, *but I jist have a feelin'*.

Her thoughts turned to Seamus. A feeling of resentment passed over her. "I could really use his help. The damn money, 'tisn't worth our bein' apart."

The week before Christmas the snow began to fall with such fury that Hannah couldn't see the old linden tree from her porch. It crept up her doors during the night and drifted past the first-floor windows. Still it continued.

The snow piled up high, often in twelve-foot drifts from Big Savage Mountain clear across to Warrior Mountain. Even Indian Will couldn't move off his mountain. So the anticipation and dreams of being together froze in time. Christmas would be a day of loneliness and disappointment.

Padraig Malone adjusted the fit of his snowshoes, threw the haunch of venison over his shoulders, and trudged a difficult five miles down Broad Hollow to Hannah's cabin. He entered through the gabled attic window bearing his gift of food.

The first Hannah knew of his arrival was the thudding sound overhead as he stomped the snow from his boots. Hannah's first thought was that the roof was collapsing from the weight of the snow. Shock was followed by delight as she watched her father-in-law climb down the ladder laden with venison.

"The wife and I couldn't have you and the twins alone on this holy day. 'Tis too difficult a walk for her. She knew I would make it."

Hannah burst into tears and hugged him. For the first time, she felt full inclusion into the Malone clan.

It took a while, but Padraig managed to dig down to the front door, over to the barn to check Whiplash, and then to the wood pile. He brought armloads in and soon the cooking fire was blazing.

The cabin was filled with delicious smells of roasting venison and root vegetables. Hannah set the long wooden plank table with her mother's china and placed pinecones and greens around the oil lamp. As darkness fell and dinner was served, the old oil lamp cast shadows that danced merrily on the cabin walls.

Mellowed by sips from Padraig's flask of potcheen, Hannah and Padraig began trading stories from their youth. Mairéad and Connor were passed from one lap to the other and bounced about until warmth and soft, lilting voices sent them into deep sleep. The stories continued late into the night.

Padraig spoke of a giant in Ireland who built a bridge of large boulders clear across to Scotland and of handsome Oisin, who went to the magical land of Tir na n-Og with the beautiful Niamh.

Accompanied by her dulcimer, Hannah sang of the tragic love of Barb'ry Allen. She remembered how she had first met Seamus and how their voices became one as they sang this song. It was difficult for her to keep the tears hidden.

"Padraig, ya must have some wonderful tales to tell of Seamus from when he was very young. Please tell me one."

Padraig obliged by telling that as a little child, Seamus ate a whole blackberry pie, denied the deed to his mother, all the while standing in front of her with berry juice smeared all over his face. He couldn't figure how she knew, and for most of his youth thought his mother had some unexplained magical powers.

Hannah laughed so hard her sides ached. She thought, *Seamus hasn't changed that much. Fer a really bright man, he sometimes still misses the obvious.*

A sharp pang of longing for Seamus filled Hannah. Except for missing him terribly, this had to be the best Christmas ever.

Seamus was bitterly disappointed that the snow had prevented him from being with Hannah and the twins. It would be another three months before the tracks were finished to Cumberland, maybe longer if the snow kept coming.

Sitting on his bunk, drinking a bowl of soup with a group of other men, was not what he had planned. Now he wasn't sure the money was worth this harsh separation. He felt his guilt grow stronger.

"'Tis too much snow. How is Hannah darlin' doin'? Are the twins warm? How big they must be now. Will they remember me?"

Oh, how very much he longed for Hannah.

The River

For millions of years, the sea bottom trough filled slowly with plant life, rising full, compressing, sinking from its own weight, making room for more organic debris. The repetitive cycle continued. Over eons, the continents drifted, collided, and the dark rock sediment buckled high into the air. Mountains formed. Springs burst into the sunlight. Rivers tumbled, gouging valleys and falls as the water returned to the ocean.

As ancient time passed, the once tall, ragged mountains gentled into verdant undulating ridges separated by deep hollows and valleys. The Potomac River, formed from erupting springs, eroded, deepened, and smoothed the land as it picked its own course. Unpredictable, it ran straight, doubled back on itself like a lunging and whipping snake.

In the sunlight or moon glow, the river, with deep glistening pools of mirrored water, could appear tame and gentle. But sometimes, unexpectedly, its powerful life blood flexed and overwhelmed all in its path. The river's own rage redefined and formed new boundaries.

Other rivers and streams blended with its waters like the harmonies of a song. The Savage, Patterson, Cacapon,

Opequon, Shenandoah, Catoctin, Tuscarora, Monocacy joined the Potomac as it crescendoed, cascading down Great Falls. The Anacostia, Piscataway, Accotink, Occoquan, Piccowaxen, and Wicomico merged into the symphonious brew, flowing into the Chesapeake Bay.

Finally, at journey's end, the churning fusion of living waters returned to the thundering, primordial ocean.

The Flood
1846

The short rails between Mount Savage and Cumberland were completed sooner than expected. By March, the spring thaw was well under way, and Seamus sent word to Hannah that he was coming home to stay.

"Remember, Hannah, darlin', the old shack at the sharp turn on Dan's Run trail? 'Tis the one right near the river where we picnicked with the twins. Be there with the buckboard Tuesday afternoon. 'Tis me hope to be in yer arms sometime before dusk."

Hannah tucked the letter in her dress next to her heart. She wanted him close to her, and this was the best she had.

Seamus rode the short rail train to Cumberland and hitched a ride on a meat delivery wagon traveling to the inn at Patterson Creek. The roads were muddy from the thaw and travel was frustratingly slow. The wheels on the wagon continued to bog down in the deep ruts. After three attempts of digging and pushing produced nothing more than failure, Seamus wished the man luck and set off on foot. Patience was never his strong point. He felt a need to keep moving toward Hannah.

At the ford in the creek, water was quickly rising. Seamus was knocked off balance. After being washed a few yards downstream, he grabbed a downed tree branch, pulled himself onto the slippery bank, emptied his shoes of water, and cussed.

"Jaysus, I'm bein' a fuckin' arse agin. May the blessed saints turn this land into a desert. 'Tis not me plan to look like a drowned rat when first I see Hannah, darlin'. Least she'll be dry inside the shack."

He was disgusted that the weather was so foul, and foul was his mood.

His right leg ached as he limped up the first steep hill. Often that troublesome leg would give him problems when he was cold, and the wet didn't help matters. Just as he topped the ridge, the dark gray, ominous clouds opened, sending down a pummeling, drenching rain. Just one more ridge to go, and he'd be with Hannah and the twins.

Seamus looked down toward the Potomac in disbelief. It was full from the thaw as expected, but charging down the river from its narrow point between the tall cliffs was an enormous wall of water. It took down trees, tumbled rocks, and roared as it came. Seamus was safe on the ridge top, but Hannah, she was in the flats.

Hannah tied Whiplash and the buckboard to an old chestnut tree. It wasn't too far from the shack where Seamus would soon arrive. The tree might provide some shelter from the rain that was beginning to pour down.

She returned to the shack to make sure Mairéad and Connor were still contented to play on the old worn coverlet. Her son had a small whittled horse that he trotted around the designs in the blanket. Her daughter was busily stacking kindling sticks, making a cabin for her corn-shuck doll. The shack had been swept to keep the grime and vermin away from the children. Hannah wanted Seamus to see them clean and at their very best. She was so proud of them.

The sound was startling. It couldn't be the train. It didn't pass by at this time of day. Hannah ran to the door and looked out in horror. A widening wall of water was coming down the flats, covering the tracks and pushing tree debris and boulders with it.

Whiplash was up to his hocks in swirling water, and it was rising rapidly. Hannah shut the shack door and raced toward the buckboard. She knew there wouldn't be enough time to unhitch the mule, so she would untie him and lead him up toward the high ground behind the shack.

Whiplash brayed and wouldn't follow Hannah. He was terrified as the water crept farther up his legs. Hannah tugged and pulled. She had forgotten to bring the carrots. In the excitement of seeing Seamus, she had left them back at the cabin.

"Please, Whiplash, please come. Come, fer the love of God. Come!" she shouted.

The mule refused to be led to safety. The wind whipped Hannah's wet hair around, stinging her eyes. She cried in desperation. She had no choice but to leave Whiplash. The water had risen to her knees.

She struggled through the swift waters toward the shelter. Clutching a sapling, she pulled herself onto dry land. Hannah ran and grabbed her babies tightly to her breast as she watched the river rise. It hadn't reached the shack yet; maybe it wouldn't.

She prayed that the mule would be sensible and pull the buckboard toward the dry land. *Dear God, please give him sense.*

"Whiplash!" she screamed.

As she watched, the river rose above the wheel hubs on the buckboard, floating it off the ground, pulling it and the mule downstream. The buckboard slammed into a standing tree surrounded by swirling water. Whiplash was irrevocably tangled. He swam in place for a long time, struggling to keep his head above water, but he couldn't break loose.

He tired and sank beneath the swift current.

Hannah felt sick to her stomach. Whiplash was a contrary but beloved old friend.

"Oh, God, 'tis a cruel death," she cried as tears streamed down her face.

As she wiped her tears, she saw that the water had risen to the stone steps of the shack and was seeping around the sides.

Seamus raced along the second ridge, limping and stumbling, pushed onward by his own fears. As he reached the far edge, he could see the roof of the shack and farther down the river something that looked like a bobbing wagon. Then he saw Whiplash struggling. Seamus let out a wrenching cry. He knew he was too late. Hannah and the babies had drowned.

"'Tis not true, Blessed Mother. 'Tis not so. Make it not so," he shouted into the rain.

Movement caught his eye as he raced down the hill. Hannah emerged from the side of the building with two bundles in her arms. They saw each other at the same time. She slipping and sliding up the hill, he careening down. Seamus grabbed both children and Hannah's arm and together they struggled up to the highest knoll.

Catching their breath, they turned toward the river to see the shack lurch from its foundation, fall sideways, bumping and turning as the current swept it away. Seamus and Hannah huddled on the ground, holding each other and the twins tightly. They both wept. They wept for the joy of finally being together. They wept for the terror they had felt, for Whiplash, for lost time, and for the pure discomfort of drenching rain.

The rain stopped as abruptly as it had begun. The sun shone through the clouds, glinting on the raging water. The river's wrath gradually subsided, somehow appeased, leaving in its wake scattered, banked debris and tree-boned remains.

The Speculators

It was a hot August afternoon when Granny Sare headed toward the young Malones' cabin. It had been over three years since the twins had been born, and the old midwife was eager to see them. Especially that boy child whom no one expected. Granny smiled to herself. "I always have da soft spot for de runt of the litter."

She walked down the path, leading Jacob, her old wether she used in place of a pack mule. Strapped to him were baskets and colorful yarns. She had come to barter them for one of Hannah's woven blankets. To the left of the old linden tree was the vegetable patch. Bright red tomatoes shone in the sunlight. Hannah and the twins were in the garden.

With dark brown curls, Connor favored his mother. Slightly smaller in build than his sister, he seemed to make up for it with determination as he dug the large hoe into the earth. Mairéad favored Seamus in coloring. Her unruly copper hair was tied into two pigtails with yellow ribbons. She squatted by a large tomato and was tugging at it. The basket beside her was half-full of the colorful fruit. Hannah looked up with surprise when she saw Granny Sare. She smiled broadly and ran to greet her.

"'Tis happy I am to see ya. 'Tis too long a time."

Hannah hugged the old woman. "We shall sit in the shade of the linden tree and drink a cooling mug of sassafras tea. 'Tis a long visit we'll be needin'."

Seamus had left early for the mill with grain from their first harvest and wouldn't return until dark. Hannah knew he'd regret missing Granny Sare. Ever since the twins were born, she had taken on mythic proportions. She was, after all, the savior of their son and the comforter to both of them during the difficult birthing.

Hannah and Mairéad went into the cabin to bring out cups and tea. Granny Sare watched as Connor stood in the garden demonstrating his hoeing skills.

She didn't see the two men right away. When she did see them walking up the path toward the cabin, Granny Sare's blood got hot. She felt it pounding through her veins. The black woman recognized them immediately as speculators, all dressed up like city dandies in their flashy clothes. They had left their wagon along Broad Hollow and approached on foot. Connor was oblivious, fully into whacking weeds and dirt clods.

"Hey, Nigra woman. We know you're hid'n slaves." The men split up, one walking toward Connor, the other toward Granny.

De Lord musta put it dere, she thought as she reached to the ground for the garden fork.

Swiftly she turned and placed herself between Connor and the speculators, aiming the fork at the testicles of the fat one.

Hannah had begun to come out the cabin door with the tea when she saw Granny and her son. In the distance approached two men. Sensing trouble, she quickly put down the tray and whispered to Mairéad to stay back beside the fireplace. Make not a sound. She had heard that strangers were in the area, nosing around, looking for runaway slaves. It was obvious from their clothes alone, these men were not from around here.

Hannah lifted the old rifle from the top of the wardrobe. It was the same flintlock long rifle her grandfather had purchased after finishing his indentured servitude, the same one he had used in Cresap's Militia during the Revolutionary War.

Her father had taken delight in teaching her to shoot it. Indian Will had continued to train her, fearing for her, as her father sickened. There were dangers around, more than hungry animals in the forest.

Carefully, Hannah poured the powder into the measure, then into the muzzle of the gun, tapping the butt onto the floorboards to settle the powder. She placed the patched ball into the barrel and, using the ramrod, firmly seated the ball against the powder. In a minute the rifle was loaded and the flash pan primed.

Hannah burst out the cabin door with the rifle, aimed at the tall, thin speculator.

"Stop where ya are. I'll shoot to kill. Which one of ya wants to die?" she shouted.

Everyone knew she had just one shot. Hannah looked menacing and held the gun steady. The men were armed with single-shot derringers.

They were familiar with the long rifle pointed at them. It had become famous during the Battle of New Orleans in 1812 when a regiment of Kentucky men routed the British. So fierce were they that they were referred to as half horse and half alligator. Since then, the gun was commonly known as the Kentucky long rifle. It was amazingly accurate at a distance, whereas a pistol was only good at close range.

Connor remained behind the large bulk of Granny Sare, as the air crackled with tension. Decisions had to be made rapidly. They could easily kill the black woman, but it wasn't her they wanted. The money was in the escaped slaves they were certain she was hiding. Dying for a Nigra was hardly worthwhile.

The thin man blurted, "Ma'm, we don't mean you no harm."

Gradually they lowered their derringers, stepped backward, turned, and rapidly left down the path toward Broad Hollow.

Granny grabbed Connor and ran for the porch steps. The women fell into each other's arms, trembling from the confrontation. Connor clung to Hannah's leg, frightened. Mairéad peered out the window and then joined the huddle on the front porch.

"Thank God for the old flintlock," said Hannah.

"Thank ya, Jesus," intoned Granny Sare.

Abolitionist newspapers had made their way through the Potomac Highlands. Slavery was a hot topic of conversation in roadhouses as well as in homes. Seamus and Hannah were decidedly against slavery. Both came to the issue with histories steeped in the fight for human dignity. It was further cemented into their psyches by their love for Granny Sare. They had long suspected that Granny needed all those blankets for more than herself.

So on the day the speculators were driven off, Hannah volunteered to make, for free, as many blankets and shawls as the black woman could provide yarn for.

Granny Sare accepted.

The Secret

Granny shook the leather bucket, which had been partially filled with dried corn.

"Sheep, come," she called, and from the small hill pasture, they raced toward her.

The late afternoon autumn air was crisp, a harbinger of a cold night to follow. Did the sheep seem agitated, or was it her finely honed senses that made the woman sing out the warning?

Her rich contralto voice sang out clearly, echoing off the hills, sounding much like an ancient spiritual. "Ye Canaan sheep, git ye to yer beds. Ye Canaan sheep git along, lie down and rest yer weary heads."

To an observer, the black woman seemed to sing for herself and the sheep. But those in hiding understood the warning and were already leaving the quaint wattle and daub hut. They quickly slid over the boulder into the hidden space. Granny hoped they would hear her in time. She wasn't sure she was being followed by more than her sheep, but she sensed danger in the cool air.

The speculators, the very same two men who had followed her to Hannah's three months ago, were close behind as the sheep streamed, bumping and pushing each other through the narrow gate leading to their pen. Beyond was the flock's reward of hay and grain, and they were eager.

Goliath, the wolf dog tethered near the gate, tensed. He growled, showing his hackles and sharp fangs, as one of the speculators attempted to peer into the pen. The dog lunged and came close to connecting with the man, but the tether stopped him short. The man backed away in fear. Goliath again lunged, breaking the rope. The derringer exploded and with a yelp, the dog fell to the ground, dead. Shaken, the speculator left to look elsewhere.

His partner had already grabbed the old woman and held a knife against her throat. Together they tied her arms and feet to a hickory tree and began to search her small hut.

They stuck knives in the haystack, hoping to find the escaped slaves. When there were no cries, they set the hay on fire, just to make sure. Then for pure spite, they lit fire to the wattle and daub dwelling. Nothing would make Granny Sare confess to slaves hiding in these hills. Her eyes smoldered in defiance as their knives sliced her skin. Not a sound uttered from her lips.

Seamus smelled the faint smoke as he followed the trail along Patterson Creek, then up the mountain to the old midwife's home. Cold weather was coming, and he was delivering a new batch of blankets and shawls from Hannah.

'Tis Granny Sare cookin' up a new batch of dye on the open fire, thought Seamus as the smell of smoke grew stronger.

The sight that greeted Seamus abruptly as he rounded the curve in the path caused his face to contort with anger. There was Granny, all four feet six inches of her, tied to a tree. She stood unflinching. Blood poured from cuts on her face and arms, but she made not a sound while two foulmouthed, gaudily dressed speculators poked knives at her stomach.

While her little house burned, the men laughed and taunted her.

"You're next, old Nigra woman. Ya'll be charred blacker than that skin of yers, blacker than the sticks left of yer weird shack."

A thought rapidly passed through Seamus' mind. There was no need to return to Ireland to fight for freedom. That fight needed to be fought right here.

With white hot rage that felt so familiar from his earlier years, Seamus stampeded down the path with the anger of a raging bull. He was upon the speculators like lightning. Lifting them up by the scruff of their necks, he bashed their heads together. Deftly, he wrested their knives from their grips, stripped them of their derringers, and threw the men, side by side, onto the ground.

It was at that very moment that Seamus had to decide. Should he kill them or should he not? Simply, it was all the attention and anger that would be brought upon a black woman that made him hesitate. For Granny's sake, he chose to let them go.

So groggy were they from the head bashing, they hardly noticed that their shoes had been pulled off, trousers slit and removed, until they were being kicked, bare-arsed, down the mountain. Seamus took only a few seconds to savor the sight before turning his attention back to Granny Sare.

Seamus cut the ropes that held the woman's hands and feet. She then crumpled to the soft earth.

"Sweet Jesus, ye saved me fer another day. Thank ye, thank ye, sweet Jesus. Sweet Jesus, ye kicked dere hateful arses clear down the mountain. Thank ye, Jesus."

Seamus lowered himself down onto his knees and held Granny Sare in his arms, rubbing her back until he could feel the tension release. She shuddered a quaking sigh as she looked at the fire consuming what was once her home. Soon, there would be nothing left but smoldering embers.

The fugitive slaves, two women and three men, slowly climbed out from behind the boulder in the sheep pen and quietly knelt beside Granny. They had escaped en route to the auction houses in Richmond. The plantations, farther south, were in need of slaves to work the large cotton fields. They would have brought their sellers a large amount of money. After six weeks of being pursued, hiding in swamps, rivers, and trees, they had been guided to Granny Sare. She was their link to freedom.

The low hum increased into a sad wailing sound as they rocked back and forth on their knees. The wailing turned into soulful prayers, half sung, half shouted, until all the pain felt from human cruelty was sent into the heavens. The emotional agony touched Seamus deeply and shrouded him with sadness.

"Is't fear forever a part of human life? Is't human dignity to be forever taken away from one people jist so others can puff themselves up?"

His temper flared again when Granny Sare confirmed that they were the same scoundrels Hannah had run off. "'Twas their heads I should have kicked down the mountain," lamented Seamus.

The problem remained. He still didn't know what to do with his anger. After all these years, the memory of bayoneted heads in County Cork still haunted him. God seemed downright fickle or wasn't paying attention to all the injustices being heaped upon His people.

Granny muttered, "I'll have no probl'm sharin' me sleeping quarters wid me sheep. Dey'll keep me plenty warm. I still have me outdoor cookin' shelter. Things could be worse. Least de speculators didn't find me runaways."

In the early morning, just as the sun began to glint through the colorful leaves, Granny gathered together her special group.

"We git goin' now. I'll take ye to de next stop on de railroad."

The fugitives gathered their meager belongings and, wrapped in Hannah's new blankets, started down the mountain path. The next stop would be Walnut Bottom, just down the hill from Emmanuel Episcopal Church in Cumberland. Samuel, the sexton, would be their guide on the next leg of their journey. Freedom was close, just six miles to the Mason-Dixon Line. Maybe they could make it to Canaan Land.

Seamus struggled with his anger, and Hannah waited. It took but half a day for him to bang around in his dark place and break into the light. He left quickly to do something that would make a difference.

Borrowing his father's gelding, Seamus rode from farm to farm, tavern and store, spreading the word about Granny Sare's plight. So many people were beholden to her that it wasn't long before he had what was needed. Some came to build and others guaranteed they'd make sure the speculators continued traveling south.

By the time Granny returned, a small cabin was under way. A pine bed with feather ticking, a twig rocker, a plank table, a bench, and split firewood were donated to that grand woman. After all, she was now helping in the births of many of their grandchildren's babies. It was important that she be safe and warm.

"'Tis sorry I am, Granny Sare, this cabin isn't wattle and daub. We jist didn't know how to do that," said Seamus with a twinkle in his eye.

The black woman smiled and twinkled back her response. "Seamus, dis might jist do me fine, but I'll accept yer 'pology anyhow."

Seamus noted that apologies in his middle years weren't nearly as difficult as they were when he was younger.

Before he left, Granny Sare asked him to please add his strong mordant to her special bucket.

"Well now," mused Seamus, "'tis a request I've never had. Only if ya turn yer head away, Granny. 'Tis me privacy I'll be needin'!" Deeply embarrassed, he nonetheless contributed a fine specimen.

The Drayman

The drayman's wagon was pulled by two mismatched mules. The larger of the two was dun colored and seemed to pull the heavy wagon to the right. The smaller white mule had the difficult job of trying to keep the course straight. The wagon lurched and bumped down the Greenspring Road, avoiding some ruts and falling into others.

Holding the reins was the hunched figure of a man. On his head was a shapeless, dusty black felt hat, half shading his unshaven bristled face. His mouth was set in an unchanging scowl. The years had not mellowed the anger that Jerral nurtured inside. It festered and charged throughout his being. His small, rodent eyes looked out at the world with resentment. There was not a day that the image of a bearded, fiery-haired Irishman didn't pass through his imagination.

Nightmares were common. Always the same scene over and over again. He could see the iron bar in his hand. It was a special tool that he had the blacksmith forge. His initials, JF, were stamped into the handle. In his dream, he held it raised and heaved it downward to smash the skull of the huge

Irishman. Just at the point of impact, the man evaporated. Jerral would awake shaking with anger.

His son, Zebediah, had never improved. He led a life of minimal existence, and Jerral felt cheated. He surely could use some help hauling these barrels of whiskey from one tavern to the next.

He mused how far he could stretch the contents of his barrels over the next four stops.

"Perhaps I'll add a little water. Fill out them barrels," he muttered.

The sight was a strange one, two men with shirts tied to their waists, bare feet, both hailing him from the ditch beside the road. At first Jerral thought he'd whip his mules into a fast trot and pass on by. Curiosity made him stop.

The men said they needed a ride south to Harrisonburg, fast, and of course they needed some trousers as well.

"We'll pay you handsomely if you'll oblige. We were attacked by a madman while doing our job. We can git you money when we reach Harrisonburg," implored the two strangers.

"Git in the back of the wagon. I'll take ya as far as me last stop in Romney, no further."

It was when Jerral found out that their job was chasing down runaway slaves that he decided to take them the rest of the way south. The promised money increased every time the speculators opened their mouths. Besides, it was all the same; Niggers, Micks, Krouts were all outsiders and didn't belong here. Anyone taking them away should be helped, especially if it meant filling Jerral's pocket.

A cloud of dust appeared on the horizon, kicked up by two men on horseback. They were moving fast.

"Git under the buffalo robes. Hide! Some men are coming."

Jerral recognized them as the two brothers who worked with the blacksmith in Frankfort.

"Hey, Jerral, seen any strangers on this road?"

"Nary a one. Not a soul in sight," the drayman replied.

After the riders left, the shaking speculators crawled out from under the robes.

"Seems like a posse might be out lookin' for ya," Jerral growled.

Conversation began slowly among the three men, each tentatively testing the attitude of the other. Jerral never contained for long his hatred of Negroes and all foreigners.

The speculators were encouraged by his seeming friendship and prejudices. They commenced telling in full detail their attack on Granny Sare. Jerral's laughter spurred them on in their tale.

It was when they told the part about a huge, fiery-haired man, thundering down upon them and bashing their heads, that Jerral abruptly reined in the mules. The barrels in the wagon rolled around unexpectedly, knocking the two men flat.

Jerral's eyes bulged. His face darkened with fury. "Did the man have a long beard?" he questioned.

"No," replied the shaken speculators.

"Did he limp?" thundered the drayman.

The speculators hesitated. "Not really sure, but he did seem to have a peculiar run. It happened so fast."

Jerral seethed. That man called Shay had been blacklisted. He couldn't still be in these parts. It couldn't be possible.

Family

Seamus began to think that maybe farming wasn't so bad after all. He loved the rhythm of the work as the seasons passed, the smell of newly plowed earth, the way seeds sprang from the ground and became plants. There were even times when he could just sit back and watch everything grow.

Mairéad and Connor were his own seed and seemed to change daily. He was grateful to watch it happen. Seamus had missed close to a year of their growing, so these days seemed all the more precious.

When he returned from Mount Savage, Seamus and Hannah had some rough times. To Seamus it seemed that if there were two ways of doing something, Hannah would favor the one that he didn't. She was so contrary.

However, she thought the same of him. Time apart brought about an independence of spirit born out of necessity. When they were together, it became mixed with guilt and latent anger.

While Seamus was in Mount Savage, Hannah continued to sell her woven coverlets at the Stone Hotel. She had carefully saved her money, keeping it in an old sugar tin in the pantry.

"Seamus, I finally found the chairs I want fer our table. They have beautifully carved spokes and are made of sturdy oak. I have money fer two, but at least that be a start."

Seamus looked at her peculiarily and responded, "Hannah, darlin', don't ya think it'd be better to spend it on a horse and wagon? The old chairs will hold up fer a couple more years."

"Well now, if ya had stayed at home, we wouldn't be needin' a horse and wagon." It was clear that Hannah was disappointed and angry. Recently, there had been too many of these bothersome squabbles.

"Seamus, 'tis not good fer us to argue so much. Reluctantly, I agree. T'will be the horse and wagon first, then the chairs. But if we can't stop being so contrary, perhaps we should jist go buy another mule to remind us of our own stubborn selves."

Passing time can be visited by a gracious perspective. Time is not always a wedge. Quite simply they began to laugh at themselves. There was too much wonder and delight in their lives to have it diminished by mere disagreements.

Many nights they held each other by the fire, children snuggled close by their sides, every one tucked beneath Hannah's coverlet of indigo and rose. The dancing flames and burning logs suggested creatures to their imaginations. Each tried to see what the other described.

After the twins were sound asleep, Hannah and Seamus slipped under the bedcovers of the old four-poster, entwined their naked limbs, holding on to each other, as their heartbeats merged. Seamus loved the feel of her hair and smooth skin as his hands slid down to her thighs. Hannah loved holding on to his earlobe, touching the hairs on his chest, pressing her hips against his. To each other they made themselves open and vulnerable. It felt warm and good.

The children brought out playfulness in Seamus. One time he took them down to the train tracks to watch as the train passed by. It wasn't yet in sight, so all three laid their heads on the rail to listen for the singing. It came soft and low at first, then high and strong. Mairéad and Connor squealed with delight.

That night when the twins told Hannah what the three of them had done, her eyes and words snapped at Seamus. "What ya think ye're doin'? Tryin' to git them killed?"

He enjoyed more approval when he taught the twins how to fish. It was when Mairéad finally caught her first big bass and Seamus caught nothing that pride filled him near to bursting. Connor caught fish as well, but his fascination was directed more toward Hannah's dulcimer. He seemed born to it.

The first tune he learned was "Go Tell Aunt Rhodie," so of course Seamus had to get him a pet gray goose. Seamus was still wrapped tightly around his children's young, little fingers.

It was in late October that Seamus eyed the pumpkin patch. He had remembered in Ireland, just before All Hallows' Day, he and his brother would carve faces into turnips and gourds and put candles inside. They called them jack-o'-lanterns.

The twins, Hannah, and Seamus each chose their favorite pumpkin, brought it inside the cabin, and sat on the puncheon floor beside the fire. Seamus began by telling the Irish story of Stringy Jack.

"Now, ya know that Stringy Jack was a tall, skinny, sly fellow who drank too much, made up lies, and played mean tricks on people. He was liked by no one.

"One day Jack was walkin' through the forest and met the devil. Now, Jack knew the devil had it in his mind to capture him, so Jack tricked the devil by gettin' him to climb a tree. Quickly Jack carved a cross on the tree trunk. The cross, it be so powerful that it prevents the devil from gittin' anywhere near it. The devil no could git down. 'Tis then that Jack made his bargain. He'd carve away the cross and let the devil slide ta the ground, only if when Jack died, the devil would no take his soul. The devil and Jack agreed.

"Several years later, Jack did die. Heaven wouldn't let Jack in because he had been so bad. The devil no could take him into hell because of the bargain. Stringy Jack had to wander the eternal darkness between heaven and hell ferever.

"Since Stringy Jack could no see in the dark, the devil tossed him an ember from the burnin' fires of hell. Stringy Jack placed it inside a hollowed-out turnip to keep the ember lit.

"Sometimes, late at night, 'tis Jack of the Lantern walking about, ya see, searching fer little children to keep him company."

The twins shrieked and clung to Hannah's arms.

She glared at Seamus. "Now are ya tryin' to make the young ones have nightmares?"

Seamus exploded with laughter. "Hannah, darlin', 'tis jist a spook story. There's no harm in that. We'll put our jack-o'-lanterns on the porch at night and 'tis that'll keep Stringy Jack away."

For a moment, Hannah had a peculiar feeling and shuddered slightly. It was as if she had sensed evil. Quickly she dismissed it. Seamus was right. It was only a spook story.

They sat in the warmth of the fire, scooped out the seeds, carved scary faces, and placed the lighted lanterns on the cabin porch.

Standing back under the linden tree and looking toward the cabin, they knew Old Stringy Jack wouldn't dare come near.

The Fight

The Chesapeake and Ohio Canal reached Cumberland, Maryland, in 1850 just eight years after the railroad. The celebrations were boisterous and colorful as Walnut Bottom overflowed with an ethnic mix of workers and dignitaries. Many people still favored shipping goods by canal boat over rail train. Still, there were dreams of continuing the canal over the Alleghenies through an elaborate system of locks that would effectively "flatten" the mountains. Both canal and railroad had plans to reach the Ohio River to open up rich commerce with the West.

The Allegheny Mountains presented a huge obstacle. Some thought, with enough determination and expendable immigrants, anything was possible.

Hannah had expected they would take Mairéad and Connor to the canal celebrations, but Seamus uttered an abrupt "No." It surprised her, but when she looked into his green eyes, she saw the pain he still harbored from his brother's death.

In reality it was more complex. Seamus liked his world now, and very few people knew he had ever been a part of the canal troubles. He didn't want to be recognized. He wanted no reminders.

The year after Seamus was blacklisted, conflicts at the canal grew worse. Retribution followed. The Washington County militia shot ten Irishmen, demolished fifty shanties, and arrested scores. Fourteen men were convicted, most of them sent to the penitentiary. It was believed that finally the Irish spirit was pacified, or more honestly said, crushed.

Seamus was a railroad worker. That was the identity he chose, not a canawler and, deep down, not a farmer.

Spurred on in part by the canal's approaching arrival in Cumberland, the rail line was well on its way through Piedmont as it followed the flatland along the North Branch of the Potomac.

But what lay ahead was a tortuous seventeen-mile grade up Backbone Mountain. The gradient of 2.2 percent was considered impossible by many for engines to pull their loads. Flying in the face of doubt were others who were determined to make it possible. Hundreds of workers were hired. Many were immigrant Irish.

Again, mountain whiskey was in ample supply, and there were constant problems with unruly, drunken workers. Again, fights were common place.

Eckhart sent a message to Seamus asking him to come and help. "If you are unable to do my bidding, I fear Backbone Mountain will become the unmarked graveyard for hundreds of our workers," he implored.

The memory of burying seven of his workers on the bluff overlooking the tracks along the Potomac pained Seamus greatly. No loved one would ever find their graves. They would never be properly mourned.

Seamus had experience. Maybe he could help. "'Tis a good team we make, me and Eckart." How could he turn his back on this plea? Unnecessary deaths would be a burden on his soul forever.

Yet he had meant it when he said to Hannah, "Never again." Being with her and the children was everything to him. So why was he even thinking about it?

He could not help acknowledging that an important piece of his identity was formed by the railroad, just as it was by Hannah and the children.

Seamus believed that no matter which decision he made, it would be the wrong one. He was deeply troubled.

He found Hannah removing the dutch oven from the fire coals. He nuzzled her neck and buried his face in her dark curls. Her warmth and the smell of the food was comforting. He wanted to forget he had ever received the message.

Hannah sensed something was troubling Seamus.

She set the pot on the woven table mat and turned to him. "What be the problem? Ya seem upset, Seamus."

He told her of Eckart's plea.

Hannah froze. The room seemed to whirl around, and in Hannah's head, swirling images of snow taller than the porch, cold, lonely nights, river water rising, Whiplash struggling, crawling up muddy banks with children in her arms, her heart beating so loudly.

She screamed, "Would that ya had a mistress, Seamus. How can I compete with an engine?"

She went to the table, picked up the cast-iron stew pot, and slammed it onto the floor. Food showered the table legs and Seamus' shoes. She stormed out the back door, crying her fury.

Seamus was stunned. And then he became equally furious. His blood rose and pounded in his head. Hannah hadn't even waited for his response.

"'Tis no respect she has fer me work. No respect fer the difficulties of the decision. No respect fer me," he yelled.

How could she be so selfish? He stomped out the front door of the cabin, slamming the door, and made his way to the road. His strides were long and fast. He ranted at the forest trees as if they were at fault. He shouted his hurt and anger all the way down the dusty road.

When his head began to clear, he found himself at his parents' farm. Sullenly he walked over to his father, who was hitching up the gelding to the buckboard.

Padraig Malone knew his son well. Anger emanated from Seamus, and there would be no sense in talking about it until he cooled down.

"I'll be goin' to the Stone Hotel to work barkeep for the evening. Join me, if ya like."

Seamus nodded and got in the buckboard beside his father. They passed by the knoll where his brother was buried, passed the snake-ridden rocky outcropping, passed the deep hollow, and neither said a word.

Padraig suspected this foul temper in Seamus might have something to do with Hannah.

Seamus finally broke the silence. "'Tis I jist don't understand how someone as soft and gentle as Hannah can turn into a screaming banshee."

Padraig Malone allowed as there was a lot that men didn't understand about women. "That Hannah of yers is real special. Doubt 'tis all her doin'."

The buckboard passed the old fort and turned left to the Stone Hotel.

Convergence

The tavern in the old hotel was a favorite stop for the wagoneers heading from Winchester to Cumberland, then onto the National Road toward Ohio. Inside, the fireplace crackled and warmed the thick stone walls. Whiskey was the preferred drink. Occasionally a local fiddler would stop by to play the discordant tunes familiar in the mountains. Fast jigs would encourage those bone-weary travelers who had enough drink to get up and dance. It was a convivial place to exchange news and stories from their travels.

Seamus noted that Sanford Staggers, the fiddler from New Creek, was sitting at the small table beside the large stone fireplace. His fiddle was resting on his lap. Sanford was the area's favorite musician. He was remarkable in that he could sing and play at the same time unlike other fiddlers who would stop the bow, sing a few lines, the resume playing.

A true gift it'll be to hear him play, thought Seamus.

At least for the moment, Seamus put aside his troubles. His attention turned to the wagoneer beside him.

"Where ya be from and where ya goin' to?" inquired Seamus.

"Been in Richmond, pickin' up cotton bales fer Baltimore, Cumberland and over to Pittsburg. Then I take any runaway slaves back to Richmond fer the speculators," the man replied.

"How kin ya take payment fer dealin' in people's lives? 'Tis a terrible evil ya do," responded Seamus.

The wagoneer looked sheepishly about the room. "It isn't what I be doin' fer real. I take the runaways a bit south. Then in the night, they mysteriously disappear. I git the money and they git a second chance fer freedom."

"'Tis not a long life ya will be havin'," said Seamus. Both men smiled.

It was then that Jerral, the drayman, came through the side door to survey the clientel. Immediately, his eyes fixed on the copper-haired man deep in conversation with a wagoneer. He wasn't sure. Without a beard, Seamus looked much younger than the rabble-rouser from the canal. He didn't look as huge as Jerral remembered. Perhaps it wasn't Shay.

After delivering the whiskey, Jerral worked his way toward the tall Irishman and observed him. Seamus wasn't aware of Jerral. The drayman wasn't anyone he had particularly given much notice to, now or before.

Sanford, the fiddler, stood up and walked to the front of the fireplace. Conversation in the room quieted to a soft murmur, as he drew the instrument to his chin. He began playing a haunting and mournful tune. To Seamus it sounded familiar, perhaps even Irish. Many of the old tunes had made their way to the mountains with the Irish settlers. The tunes changed, but often one could recognize bits and pieces from the old country. Then it struck him. This tune was a variation of "My Lagan Love", the song he had sung many years ago for the men at the Paw Paw Tunnel.

This time, instead of being a veiled song about the beloved homeland of Ireland, it was clearly about a flesh and blood, passionate woman.

'Tis about me Hannah, darlin'.

When Seamus had his second whiskey, he couldn't get Hannah out of his mind. He loved her so much.

'Tis not good to walk away from the troubles. 'Tis not good fer either of us.

Seamus rose from his chair and told his father he needed to go back home. Padraig agreed.

Jerral watched as Seamus moved out the door. He saw the slight irregular walk. He saw the limp. Fury consumed him.

"That's him! The murderous bastard of me nightmares. Finally, I've found him," he fumed.

Jerral decided to follow.

The walk would be a long seven miles home. The full moon shone brightly, lighting the way. The air was crisp and invigorating. Seamus was full of hope. Hannah and he would figure out their differences together. She was special, more special than anyone in this world to him.

Jerral felt that Lady Luck was finally on his side. The man he hated was walking down Dan's Run. No one else was in sight. He pulled his wagon away from the Stone Hotel and followed for a while at a distance.

Pulling alongside Seamus, Jerral called out, "We're goin' in the same direction. I'll give ya a ride."

Seamus thanked the drayman and climbed in the wagon. The sooner he got back to Hannah, the better.

"Ya from around these parts? Name's Jerral. Who might ya be?"

The answer came back, "Seamus, live down Broad Hollow."

Jerral could barely breathe. *Shay.... Seamus. This is the man of me fuckin' nightmares. There's no doubt.*

"I'm goin' to the inn at Patterson Creek. Drop ya off at Broad Hollow."

"'Tis a kindness," answered Seamus.

Not much was said as the wagon pulled up to Broad Hollow. Seamus could have noticed the tension in Jerral, but he was too caught up in what he would say to Hannah.

Seamus thanked the drayman and turned to step down from the wagon. He landed on his weak right leg and stumbled forward.

It was just at that moment that Jerral attempted to slam his forged iron bar full force onto Seamus' skull. The blow glanced off its mark, but nonetheless hit soundly enough, knocking Seamus unconscious, facedown onto the dirt road. Blood quickly dampened the earth.

The drayman felt a surge of adrenaline, intoxicating joy. The Irishman hadn't evaporated as in his dreams.

Quickly he heaved the body onto the wagon, threw the iron bar alongside, and whipped the mules toward the tracks at the bend by the river. He would make the death look like an accident. It would be a long while before they'd even be able to recognize his victim.

Jerral checked his pocket watch. He knew the train came by at 9:20. He passed that way often. It would be coming soon. Hurriedly, he dragged Seamus off the wagon and onto the tracks. Jerral put his ear on the rail and could hear the distant train approaching. He breathed out with satisfaction, "It's on time!"

As he leapt onto his wagon, he figured he had about four minutes to disappear.

He whipped the mules into a full gallop and headed back the way he had come. It wouldn't be good to be seen anywhere nearby. He'd take the shortcut down Broad Hollow to Oldtown. He laughed loudly, exhilarated by this long-awaited vengeance.

Hannah felt embarrassed and disgusted with herself. She cleaned the stew from the floor and table legs. Mairéad and Connor looked at her with doleful eyes. They were upset by their mother's crying and didn't understand why their father had left.

"Sometimes parents act very bad, even spoiled. 'Tis me temper I lost with little chance fer yer Da to speak. I am sorry. I will apologize to yer father. It'll be all right. You'll see." Hannah held the children tight, trying to soothe away their fears.

Late that evening, Hannah sat alone on the cabin porch, waiting for Seamus to return. In the moonlight, she could see the distant road. The cool air smelled of wood smoke from her chimney. In the distance, she could hear the familiar sound of the train.

Another sound, that of a wagon and fast hoofbeats, grew louder. Hannah saw the swift passing of the drayman. It seemed odd. He had not traveled that way before, and what was his hurry?

Her attention went back to the steady rumble of the train. Suddenly, there was a loud screeching of metal crashing against metal, echoing throughout the hollows. Hannah's heart skipped several beats. She knew there was something terribly wrong.

The drayman reached the fork in the road and turned left toward Greenspring. The mules were tiring from their fast pace, so he reined them in. He felt so good, even magnanimous toward the mules. In fact, he had never felt so good in the whole of his life. He had justice.

That Irish devil finally got what he deserved. He and his kind caused so much personal suffering. Now it's his turn.

Jerral felt light-headed and giddy. He went over and over the scene in his mind, savoring every aspect. How fine it felt to connect his iron bar with the bastard's skull. That special iron bar the blacksmith had made. His favorite tool.

Jerral turned to look in the wagon bed. He'd have to be sure to clean up the blood. The bar would need attention too.

"The bar! Where is it?" he growled.

He halted the mules and searched the back of the wagon, searched his mind. The iron bar was missing.

Could it have fallen from the wagon when I dragged the Irishman onto the tracks?

As he suddenly remembered that his initials were on the bar, his exhilaration turned to cold sweat. His stomach felt like lead. Fear seeped into his body.

Breaking Point

His forehead lay against the cold iron rail. Slight vibrations stirred his memory. Then the white hissing tunneled him toward the pinpoint light, absorbing his consciousness. Out of the snowy darkness of his mind came the insistent vibrating hum, searing into his skull, into his mind. Children laughing, bending low, ears pressing expectantly on the iron rail. Hannah upset, making unintelligible, angry noise. All disappeared as the piercing pain seemed to split him in half, metal upon metal grating.

Terror had been the awakening force, as the bobbing light bore down upon him. Coupled with it was the shadowy primal instinct for survival. Powerful adrenaline surged through his body as Seamus began to pull himself off the tracks. He felt a searing pain on his right side as his mind swirled back into the darkness.

The engineer thought he saw something on the tracks ahead. It looked to be a pile of rags. But just to make certain, he pulled the brakes on the train.

It was too late. He recognized the hunched figure of a man, then a slight bump as the engine halted just past the body. Exiting the engine, he walked back to find a blood-soaked man. The engineer sent his two firemen in search of help.

Pigman

It was common in those days. Pigman's kin all followed the formula. After a baby was born, the mother would take the big black book, close her eyes, flip the page edges, then snap the book all the way open. Still with eyes closed, she'd point a finger on the page and pray for God's guidance to select the name for her child. This act would be repeated until an appropriate male or female name was found.

God made Pigman's mother try twenty-one times until her finger landed on the name Cain in Genesis, chapter 4, verse 15. "And the Lord said unto him, Therefore whosoever slayeth Cain, vengeance shall be taken on him sevenfold. And the Lord set a mark upon Cain, lest any finding him should kill him."

Not only was her baby protected by the Lord, but the quote also explained the small patch of discolored skin above his left eye. It was God's mark. This was good. Most people knew that a name selected from the Bible would lead the baby on a path of righteousness

Cain had first heard the story about Cain and Abel when he was seven years old. It was at his first tent meeting, and all the other kids from the nearby villages and farms were there. He was badly teased.

Smarting from this new information, he blamed his mother. In turn she was upset. She had only done what her mother had done. Her name, Martha, seemed to work just fine. Besides, she was not all that literate. She only read the Bible when she needed to name a newborn child.

Cain never liked his name after that. As he grew older, he was content to be called Pigman. It described him better. He would never kill his brother. But it still gnawed at him, that name. A name had the power to affect who you really were.

It was when he leapt upon the back of a hog, poked his sharp-pointed blade behind the jugular and forcefully pulled outward that he felt kinship to Cain. Killing was invigorating. The power he had over a beast weighing four hundred pounds or more made his heart quicken.

After the kill, he'd hang the hog, snout down, from the thick arm of the nearby elm. He'd set the old tin bucket on the ground to catch the warm blood. The smell was oddly comforting. The thought of the pudding he'd make from it made his stomach growl.

In the fall, people from town came to barter for his hogs. Once the animal was singled out in the swine pen, Pigman got to work. Some climbed and sat on the fence to watch. Others distractedly fiddled with their harness leathers, averting their eyes. It was unavoidable. They couldn't block out the terrified squeals of the pigs.

Pigman was a peaceful man despite what he did to hogs. The only other times he felt aggression was late at night under the old crazy quilt, nuzzled against the soft folds of his woman. His body would respond, growing its own blade. Often she squealed, but it was with delight. She'd meet his body as if in a fever. Again this year, she'd be wearing her apron high.

The pig farmer lived halfway between the tracks and Broad Hollow. His small log cabin, two rooms with dirt for floor, was home to his wife and six kids. It was tucked back down a hollow.

Drowsing by the fire, he awoke with a start from the insistent pounding on the door and the baying of his hounds. The two railroad men and his eldest son helped as he hitched his mule to the wagon.

"Yep, I know him. That's Seamus Malone. Red hair like that belongs only to one person hereabouts. Best thing to do is to take him to his wife. If he's not dead already, he'll soon be."

The men carefully lifted the motionless body onto the pig man's buckboard.

As he flicked the reins and the mule began to move, the engineer called out, "Wait, take this as well. It doesn't seem properlike to let the wild animals gnaw on it."

So onto the buckboard was tossed Seamus' leg. It had been severed just below the knee by the wheels of the train.

Pigman thought, *My swine fare better than this man I'm haulin'.*

Vision

Indian Will sat cross-legged in front of his cave fire. Smoke rose as he placed bundled herbs on the flames. The pungent smell filled the room as he intoned his ancient chants. He breathed in deeply. Gradually, he slid into a trance. He had felt it in his bones, a compelling need. Something was wrong. As the smoke thickened, a vision emerged out of the flames. It bespoke of red, blood, hair, raw emotion. He jolted out of the trance, filled his medicine bag, and headed toward Hannah's cabin.

At the sound of the wagon pulling in toward her cabin, Hannah grew excited. It had to be Seamus. Apprehension filled her as she saw only the shapes of Pigman and a boy. Disbelief and reality converged as Hannah peered into the wagon upon the bloody remains of her husband.

The air was heavy around her. She could hardly breathe. Her heart pounded so hard in her chest, it felt that she'd split wide open. The voice, so far away, wailing in agony, she recognized as her own.

It was after Seamus was placed on the walnut poster bed, after Pigman left, that the numbness set in, and Hannah began to quiet her cries. Did she see him twitch, see his chest rise slightly? Hannah grabbed his wrist, felt the ever-so-frail pulse. Then hope mingled with panic. What must she do? He was still alive.

Some say certain people can sense tragedy across miles, often knowing things that are impossible to know. Most everyone has experienced the unknowable or at least knows of someone who has. It is not that uncommon. But there are those who have the gift in abundance. They are blessed with an uncanny sensitivity.

Hannah had not heard him as he entered the cabin. Nor did she know how long he had stood next to her. Panic gradually turned to faith in the impossible as Indian Will quietly instructed Hannah. Bleeding must be stopped, hot water, clean cloths, cleansing the wounds. She did as he instructed, mixing powdered slippery elm bark and ground flax seeds with bear tallow, brewing a tea of wild cherry bark and honey, and using comfrey leaves and spiderwebs as binding bandages.

It was strange that what remained of his leg hardly bled at all. The heavy train wheels had cut it off just below the knee, mashing blood vessels and nerves closed. Hannah supposed it must be a miracle given the circumstances.

Will placed the severed piece of leg in an empty feed sack, bound it with twine, and hung it from the dry rafters of the old barn. Both wanted it out of the way. If Seamus died, they would bury it with him.

Seamus lay in a fitful, unconscious state. He could still hear the white hissing sound in his throbbing brain, see the pinpoint light, hear the screeching metal. The vision played over repeatedly. His arms clawed the air as if trying to pull himself into consciousness. Then all faded into stillness.

Mairéad and Connor, with huge fearful eyes, looked upon the bruised and battered man. "Mum, is Da goin' to die?" Their young voices trembled with emotion.

Four days passed before Seamus opened his eyes. He moved his mouth as if to speak, but uttered only a dry, raspy sound. Hannah held his head and encouraged sips of the cherry bark tea laced with honey. He tried to speak again. Hannah leaned close, cupping her hands gently toward his mouth.

Seamus whispered, "Hannah, darlin', I'm sorry."

Tears brimmed in her eyes. She placed her lips softly on his and kissed him over and over again.

The Disquieted Soul

The thunder rumbled in the distant hills as the wind pushed the storm closer. Rain poured down, watering the drought-ridden fields. It was a midsummer rain. Seamus brooded. He brooded most of the time these days.

Months had passed, and still he woke praying it was just a nightmare. Sometimes he was sure he felt the rest of his leg. So clearly he felt it that he'd push the bedcovers away only to find the truncated right leg glaring up at him.

He was troubled and angry. He didn't like people looking at him, not friends, not family, not even Hannah. Seamus saw only pity in their eyes, not the hurt his rejection caused.

He had felt less than a whole man two times before. First, when Connor was killed by his blast, and second, when he had walked through the angry mob in Oldtown. The bile stirred up and rose into his throat when he thought of those times.

He had never been back to the Paw Paw or Oldtown for that matter. Seamus had thought that he had left all that pain behind, except now it raced continuously through his mind. It was the unrelenting sense of his own failure, that fault within him, that tied the past pain and present horror together. He was the cause of so much misery.

To make everything worse, he had no idea why the drayman had done this to him. For Seamus, not knowing was unacceptable, impossible.

"'Tis his own head I'd like to split open, feel his skull crush under me own hands. I'd carve his limbs off one at a time 'til he's a quivering trunk. I want Jerral dead."

But the sheriff claimed he couldn't track him down. Everyone knew Jerral had done this to Seamus. The iron bar had been found with blood and strands of copper hair stuck to it. But Jerral was gone, flat disappeared. Rumors were rampant. Some thought he had gone to Ohio, drowned in the mighty Monongahela, or just was hiding up on Backbone Mountain.

The revenge that obsessed Seamus dined upon his soul. He was inconsolable and bitter. Not even his children could reach him. He seemed different. He didn't smile, wouldn't give hugs or affection. It was as if he looked through them, not at them. The internal churning emotions within Seamus paralyzed his ability to love and to accept love.

Hannah watched as Seamus harnessed his father's gelding to the buckboard, watched as he placed the old flintlock inside the gunnysack.

She remembered when she had first shown him her grandfather's rifle, told him stories of its noble past, fighting for the country's freedom. It was during that sun-filled summer, before they married, that they had entered into a spirited competition of marksmanship, shooting at tall sticks stuck in the ground. Over time, he had become as good a shot as she. Hannah had teased him that he was marrying her for the love of the old flintlock.

Now, sadly, she watched.

He moved with stubborn determination, relying on a crotched hickory stick for stability. Her own fears and sadness became mixed with anger.

"Seamus, it will do no good. Ya will become jist like that man. The hatred ya feel will be yer only reward."

He flashed back a sarcastic grin, "Devil willin', I'll git me opportunity."

He pulled out down the road, not looking back, heading straight for Oldtown. It was there he'd find some answers, perhaps a lead to Jerral's whereabouts. He'd hunt him down. The closer he got to Oldtown, the more it felt as if he were being pulled into a dark abyss.

It was late afternoon, still hot and so dry the buckboard kicked up clouds of dust as it traveled toward the Pine Tavern. Jerral, as a drayman, would be known there. He had hauled whiskey to all the taverns in these hills.

Seamus had steeled himself for an unfriendly reception. There had been no love for the Irish when he was here last. Most likely nothing had changed.

The five men at the bar turned their eyes toward the door as he walked in. It was obvious they knew who he was. The red hair and missing leg were all that was needed.

Their surprise turned to tense apprehension as the barkeep announced, "You Irish ain't served here."

Seamus continued making his way toward the bar. "'Tis not yer drink I'll be wantin'. Jist answer me one question. Why? Why'd he do this?"

The barkeep was a black-bearded, burly man, hook-nosed and slightly older than Seamus. He felt he could hold his own with a one-legged man, but the stories Jerral had told about the man called Shay made him hesitate. He glared at Seamus.

"You got what was due. Many wish ya dead," he replied.

"Why?" insisted Seamus.

"Ye're a murderous coward, shooting at a small child like that."

Seamus was speechless for a minute. "What child? When?"

All five men chimed in, spewing insults and hatred at Seamus. They spoke of a young life ruined, of how Jerral's sister had to work daily in the fields just like a slave in order to take care of an invalid and herself.

Seamus felt a strange disorientation. After all, he was the one beaten and left to die on the tracks. He was the one missing a leg.

"Who is this boy called Zebediah?" He didn't know of anyone with that name.

"Go see fer yourself, you Irish bastard. Maybe that'll jog yer memory."

Seamus retorted, "It'll snow in hell before I do that. His problems are none of me makin'."

Seamus left shaking with rage. "Why am I to blame for something I couldn't have done? I didn't carry a gun in those days. I didn't need to. This is more of the same. The Irish getting blamed for everything," he shouted.

Yet something in his memory crept forward. Gradually he began to remember. Boys with rocks, a gunshot, an injured child at the tavern, just before he was blacklisted.

He left the way he had come, heading toward Greenspring. He heard the jeers and laughter coming from the Pine Tavern as if chasing him down the road.

Once out of sight, Seamus veered to the left, taking the ancient path toward the old ford. *I'll cross over, takin' the back parallel road to the west side of town.* Despite what he had said, he wasn't about to return home with his tail between his legs. *'Tis some answers I'll be needin'.*

"Perhaps 'tis the drayman's sister who'll talk to me. And who the hell is Zebediah? 'Tis nothing I did to deserve this hate," murmered Seamus.

The German miller knew how to find the Floyds' house. He gave directions to a small whitewashed cottage just a quarter mile down the rutted road.

Sitting on the porch was a thin young man, head leaning on a hunched shoulder, hair the color and texture of straw. His eyes looked directly at Seamus.

Was there a spark of recognition? Seamus sat down on the steps, his hands resting on the hickory stick. He looked up. "Are ya Zebediah?"

There was no response, but the eyes continued to stare straight at him. Seamus wasn't sure what the boy could see or even if he could understand what was being said.

"I'm sorry fer what happened to ya. Some people seem to think 'twas me that did this. The devil be damned in hell, 'twasn't I who did it."

Zebediah still made no response. He stayed motionless, as if frozen in time.

Seamus had a sickening feeling. How awful it would be, imprisoned in such a body. He then noticed the wide leather strap that held him to the unpainted wooden slatted chair. This boy was so unlike his own lovely, healthy children.

It happened in a flicker of time. Zeb's eyes seemed to dart toward the bushes behind Seamus. The rope garroted his neck with unrelenting force as Seamus grasped at the tightening hands. In desperation, he threw himself backward on top of the man behind him. It was Jerral, and Jerral was intent on completing the job he had started.

On the ground, Seamus had just about the same fighting ability as always. It was the standing position that was difficult. He'd make sure they'd stay down. It was a fight to the finish and both knew it. Seamus gouged at Jerral's eyes, punched at his testicles until the rope loosened slightly. He slid his thumbs under the cord, taking the pressure off his windpipe, and slammed his head into Jerral's face. Blood spewed from his broken nose, and Seamus was able to take control of the rope.

With quick dexterity honed from many years of brawling, Seamus tied the rope around Jerral's neck, lashed his hands tightly behind him, and bound his legs to the cherry tree. Jerral's body thrashed about as he pleaded for mercy. A wet stain spread near his groin. His fear only fueled Seamus' lust for blood.

Reaching for his stick, Seamus hobbled over to the gunnysack on the buckboard. He came back and stood towering over Jerral. Holding the flintlock at close range, he shot the ground next to Jerral's face. Carefully loading again, Seamus explained that he was going to shatter each limb of his body, render him useless, then bash his skull in with the gun butt.

Seamus took slow, careful aim at the drayman's right leg. That would be the first to go.

Just a half second before his finger could pull the trigger, Seamus heard a chilling wail.

It reminded him of something primordial, something familiar, something about Connor. The cry was like his own, as he had watched the slabs of slate slice into his brother. He looked toward the porch and saw Zebediah's mouth wide and contorted. The sound came from him.

"Yer reward is hatred, Seamus. Ya are no better than that man." Hannah's words hit him soundly.

With trembling hands, Seamus lowered the gun. Glowering at Jerral, Seamus said, "Ye aren't worth me soul. The devil can have ya."

He left quickly before he could change his mind.

Seamus found the sheriff sleeping in the late noon's heat outside his small log office. He jumped at the sound of Seamus' voice.

"'Tis Jerral ya'll find all tied up to the cherry tree next to his house. I don't think ya looked fer him very hard."

The sun was beginning to set as Seamus followed the old Warrior's Path toward Greenspring. As thoughts sifted through his brain, a realization began to formulate. Like pieces of a puzzle making sense out of shapes and colors, his thoughts interlocked,

'Tis hate that made me family flee Ireland. 'Tis hate that made boys throw rocks. 'Tis hate that made Jerral try to kill me. 'Twas hate that almost turned me into a murderer.

Three lives had been changed forever by hate. Jerral would spend a long time in prison, no doubt. Seamus would forever be physically maimed. Yet it was Zebediah, the one most damaged, who had saved them both. His wail had saved Jerral's life, and surprisingly, it saved Seamus from his own destructive revenge.

Chills spread over his body as he recalled ancient tales of the wounded healer, primitive tales of suffering that empowered forgiveness. He wasn't close to forgiving, but he felt a stirring of life within him, a feeling his emotionally deadened self hadn't allowed for a long while.

It will be good to return to Hannah.

A Wake

It was the old linden tree that finally caught his attention. Last summer it had been hit by lightning. A large branch near the top had split off from the force of the strike. This summer, despite the drought, new branches partially covered the wound. Seamus felt a pang of envy. He wished he could heal like the tree. Wished, like a new branch, his leg would grow back.

The spirit can wallow around in darkness only so long before it must decide to die or live. He had decided that day in Oldtown to live.

Using his hickory branch as a crutch, Seamus worked his way to the wood shop. The sun shone through the window by the bench table, casting a warm glow on the set of wooden chisels. He picked them up, one by one, feeling how their rounded shape fit into his palm. It felt soothing and exciting altogether.

Working the piece of oak was more difficult than he had anticipated, but he whittled away until it took the shape he wanted. Using strips of hide and fleece for padding, he'd design a way to attach it.

Hannah watched as each day Seamus awkwardly made his way to the shop. All he said was he had some work to do. He seemed happier, especially when he returned. Whatever he was up to, he'd let her know when he was good and ready.

'Tis workin' well, thought Seamus.

He practiced up and down, turning, a fast walk, even a hop. He loved having both hands free. But he knew there was more to do.

Taking the smallest chisel, he began carving a fish rising upward. It was the symbol of the Salmon of Wisdom from Irish lore. Perhaps he would take on some of its wisdom. He surrounded the fish with spirals, representing ocean, symbols of Stone Age mystery.

"'Tis me life. 'Tis filled with mystery," mused Seamus.

Top and bottom were ringed with intricate knot work representing interconnected life and eternity. Then he rubbed it with tallow and the grain took on warmth. The warmth then spread through him as he turned it over in his hands. The Irish lore, his history, his dreams were carved into this piece that would soon become part of him. The ancient stories and symbols would hold him upright.

In the half moonlight, the whip-poor-wills were singing. Hannah was on the cabin porch with Connor. In her hand was the dulcimer.

"'Tis the Aeolian tuning I'll be showin' ya. It makes the most mysterious sound. Jist press the bottom string right here. Make the first two strings sound jist like it," instructed Hannah.

While Connor was attempting the new tuning, Mairéad raced around the garden catching lightning bugs, only to let them fly free again.

Hannah was just beginning to teach a new modal tune to Connor when she became aware of movement close by. She looked up and gasped.

"Seamus, how can this be!" exclaimed Hannah.

Seamus had silently walked over to the porch. There he stood smiling. His arms were outstretched, and he held no crutch. He moved back and forth, teetered a bit, regained his balance, and ran a few steps. It was an amazing feat, but it was really the broad smile that made their hearts sing.

"'Tis the healing, the blessed healing. 'Tis the beginning," she whispered to herself.

The feed sack had stayed in the rafters of the old barn, shrouding its strange relic. Will had told them what he had done, but no one wanted to do anything about the leg. Out of sight but not quite out of mind. The dry air from the summer drought had shriveled what remained of the limb.

Hannah, balanced on a tall ladder, retrieved the feed sack from the rafters and handed it to Seamus. He was surprised at how heavy it was but declined to look inside. Seamus had decided the leg needed to be buried. In his mind, no one, or precisely, no piece of one, should be buried without an Irish wake.

It gave Hannah an uncomfortable feeling to have the leg hanging over their heads anyway. The symbolism didn't escape either of them.

"Seamus, if it takes an Irish wake to bury yer leg, then so be it." Hannah recognized that it was more than a leg being buried.

The children helped Seamus build a small wooden box for the coffin, while Hannah went to the garden to fetch the remaining corn, tomatoes, and squash. Together with a few potatoes and the last of the smoked venison, she'd put together a tasty stew. Corn bread and apples for pie from the tree behind the cabin would make a fine feast.

As she lit the fire, smoke moved up the chimney. With it were carried Hannah's prayers for a renewed family life.

Only special people were invited to the night's wake. Both knew that more than a few would consider it a bit daft. Deirdre and Padraig came to support their son, hoping that the nonsense of a wake for a leg would further pull him out of his depression. Indian Will, Granny Sare, and the children completed the gathering.

The wooden box sat near the hearth surrounded by wildflowers the children had picked. Black-eyed Susan, Queen Anne's lace and cornflower were lovingly arranged.

As the sun set and the flask of potcheen was passed, stories of the dearly departed ones began to be told. Some stories were sanguine, some sad, some scary, and even some hysterically funny.

"'Tis me favorite, I think," said Hannah. "'Tis the four pallbearers slippin' on the rain-soaked grass, fallin' into the freshly dug grave, bringin' the coffin down on top of them."

Actually she was not sure. "Perhaps 'tis the one about the elderly man bendin' down to place a flower on the coffin, havin' his false teeth pop out and skitter down the side. 'Twas good as well. Fer sure, Connor laughed the loudest at that."

Indian Will just shook his head knowing somehow all this laughter would be healing.

Granny Sare had never drunk liquor of any kind, but since she was among friends, she'd just try a small sip. The potcheen stung and burned her throat as it inched its way clear down to her belly. Then the warmth spread throughout her body in a most delightful way.

Three long sips later, the room seemed to rock a bit, but it was after the fourth that Granny Sare burst into song, her rich deep voice singing "Swing Low, Sweet Chariot." When she substituted "comin' for to carry de leg home" for the proper words, laughter, uncontrollable laughter, filled the room.

Even the serious Indian Will allowed himself a chuckle.

Seamus was pleased with the wake. There was something satisfying, laughing in the face of his own personal pain.

As the mist on the hills began to burn off and dew sparkled on the webbed grass, the tiny group gathered with solemnity at the Malone family cemetery. Seamus had chosen a site near an old oak tree just down from where his brother was buried. Carefully he placed the box in the hole, and all four, Seamus, Hannah, Mairéad, and Connor pushed the dirt on top.

After standing silently for what seemed a respectful time, Hannah turned to Seamus. "I need ya to make me a promise."

"Hannah, darlin', I will if I can," replied Seamus.

Hannah looked directly and deeply into his eyes, the corners of her mouth twitching with humor.

"I need ya to promise me that when I die, ya'll bury me next to yer grave site, not next to yer leg. Seamus, 'tis nothing to come between us, not even yer leg."

He held her close. "Hannah, darlin', 'tis me promise."

Chrysalis

Life began to take on a steadiness that had long been missing. Hannah still wove her intricate coverlets to sell at the Old Stone Hotel, even sending some to Hagerstown by rail for her sister, Leah, to market in the General Dry Goods Store. After each sale Hannah put half away toward the purchase of a horse and wagon. Since the terrible flood that killed Whiplash and destroyed the wagon, they had borrowed Padraig and Deidre's buckboard and gelding for necessary transportation. That was not easy for the independently minded Hannah. She was content that her chairs would be purchased at a later time.

Seamus became absorbed in the wood shop, carving intricate panels of knot work. The old Celtic designs began to appear on their mantels, staircases, porch railings, table legs, even their four-poster bed. It was when a large slab of pine, carved like a shield, appeared on their front door that Hannah decided they needed to have a serious talk.

"Seamus, me love, would ya mind terribly if ya tried makin' me the chairs I've always wanted? I do think we have enough of yer lovely knot work. Sometimes I feel as if I'm livin' inside one."

It was a gentle enough request for Seamus to hear, but the fact was, he knew the Windsor chairs that Hannah loved required more skills than he had. Her comment, even though lovingly said, did sting a bit. Seamus enjoyed carving those designs. Each knot, whether of a fish, dog, or person, spoke of life being connected to all of creation. It was a spiritual thing that he did.

As he pondered how to respond, Seamus looked around at all the carvings and then at the crude, rustic chairs by the table. Maybe it was time to do something about those chairs that Hannah had wanted for so long.

"Perhaps the old chair maker near Patterson Creek could take me on as his apprentice, because, Hannah, darlin', ya wouldn't be wantin' to sit in any chair I could make."

When the two men met, there was an unmistakeable easiness between them. Seamus became an able apprentice of Emrock, the chair maker. Slowly Seamus produced his first Windsor. It was meticulously made, and the master chair maker breathed a sigh of relief. At long last, here was someone to help with the many back orders, someone to take over the work when Emrock retired.

The men worked well as a team. Seamus was able to make money enough for some of the things they had gone without. Together Hannah and Seamus bought a wagon and a large gray gelding from a farmer in Romney, and gradually, one by one, Hannah got her chairs. Seamus had not been this happy in many years.

It was a shock, on that chilly fall morning, to find Emrock dead on the shop floor, splayed out among the logs he had carried in for the fireplace.

The doctor concluded, "It was probably his heart that gave out."

A good friend had been lost, but Emrock would continue to live on in the skills passed to Seamus. He bought from Emrock's wife the old shaving horse and draw knife and set up shop in the small log building Hannah's father had used. People already knew and respected Seamus' skills. The business flourished.

These were the best of times.

The Challenge
1854

Hannah's long hours weaving gave her plenty of thinking time. The twins attended the one-room school off Dan's Run Road during the weekdays. In a way she missed their interruptions that made her lose count on her treadles. She even had left a mistake on Connor's birthday coverlet so she could forever remember the twins' big day.

Her mind wandered further. Near their school were the graves of the railroad workers that Seamus said were marked with small river rocks.

That railroad, she thought. *What misery it brought to some.*

Her mind couldn't help returning to the terrible night when Seamus was brought to her cabin, presumed dead. Then to Jerral.

Why is he so hateful? Why?

That young man called Zebediah; it is unfair what has happened to him. How fortunate are our children.

Seamus had told her that it was the boy's wail that had stopped him from killing Jerral.

Hannah had never seen Zebediah, and it troubled her.

What kind of life does he have? He must have understood somethin' of what was happenin', or was the wail just a random sound? Is he still lashed to a chair like a poor animal while his aunt goes off to work?

The more Hannah mulled over the scenes and questions in her head, the more she couldn't leave them alone. *I have to go see Zebediah.*

Of course there would be an argument. Each knew the stubbornness of the other. But the rules had changed. No one was to leave in anger.

"Never will I go back to Oldtown, Hannah, and 'tis I who forbid ya to go. Jist look at what happened to me."

"Seamus, Jerral was taken to prison. The people in that village know 'tisn't acceptable to beat one senseless and toss him on the tracks. Surely they're glad he is gone. Ya could have killed him but ya didn't. What of Zebediah? I need to see if we can do some small thing fer him."

"I don't owe him anything. 'Twas I trying to stop a riot that night when he got injured. 'Tis none of me doin'."

"Ya left Ireland because of hate and cruelty. One group claiming rights over another. Putting heads on pikes. Others jist standing by and watching. What makes us different, Seamus? Ya were right to try and stop the violence, and I believe that 'tis right fer us to show a little compassion to an innocent boy."

"'Tis a bit late, Hannah."

"It well may be, Seamus, but I need to try."

"I can't go back, Hannah."

"I'll take Indian Will. I know how difficult it must be for ya. I promise, I will be careful."

There was a long silence.

"Seamus, I love ya. Thank you."

Trapped

What people did not understand about Zebediah was that while he was partially paralyzed and could not string words together in the usual way, he could think. He understood the world around him. Words were sparse and took enormous effort to say. But there wasn't anyone there to listen anyway. He was trapped in his own body, not just because the bullet had passed through the left side of his brain, but also in part because of what others thought. Some viewed him as their village idiot, totally incapable of thinking and making even the slightest sense. No one thought to ask him if he could understand words, let alone say them.

To her credit, Jerral's sister, Flora, continued to take care of the boy. She worked hard at any job she could find. Survival was difficult, and she had little energy left for Zebediah. It was a great kindness when someone from the village stopped by with food or discarded clothing. In the mornings, Flora would feed him porridge, strap Zeb to the strong plank chair with Jerral's old leather belt, and leave for the fields to harvest the newest crop. Sometimes it would be apples, other times peaches, corn, or berries, depending on the season.

For extra money she would take in clothes for washing. She'd work in the evenings, beating the wet clothes on the battling bench with a wooden paddle to loosen the dirt, then boil them in water with lye soap until clean. People nearby could hear the soft thudding of the paddle late into the night. There was precious little time for that. Certainly not on God's day when she would attend church, praying for something, anything better.

Flora meant well. But for Zeb, the pain and humiliation he had experienced for most all of his young years came back to him each time he was strapped to the chair. It was that belt, the same belt his Pap had used to cut him so cruelly.

Family ways often get passed on for generations. Sometimes it's an ugly legacy; other times it's not so bad. Flora, like Jerral, knew the lash of the belt from their parents. The belt gave power over the unfortunate. It was used freely when tempers flared. The belt could be unbuckled and whipped off the body in seconds, a tool, a visual threat. Flora only did what Jerral had done. They only did what their parents had done to them.

After being lashed to the chair for long hours, Zebediah, sometimes, could hold back no longer and would mess his pants. Flora would be furious and strap him hard on his back with Jerral's belt. It was all the exhaustion and frustration she felt that made her temper explode.

"I don't like doin' the whippin', but what am I supposed to do? I turned out all right." Yet her gut roiled, and she knew deep down, something was wrong.

Zebediah felt he was already in the burning fires of hell. He had heard them talked about when Flora read the Bible.

The Meeting

Seamus watched as Hannah and Indian Will left for Oldtown. He knew that Will wouldn't let anything happen to her, but just the same he felt a white flash of fear. It sent a shock into his head that momentarily blinded him. He shook his head, and it was gone as fast as it had come. Yet his pulse was still beating fast.

He chided himself. "'Tis the fear that's mine. 'Tis not something to do with Hannah."

Hannah knocked on Flora's door. No one answered. Her second knock was more forceful and jarred the door partially open. Still no answer. Perhaps they were gone, and her trip was just a waste of time. The basket on her arm felt heavy. It was filled with smoked ham, turnips, carrots, butter, fresh-baked bread, and an apple pie.

Hannah thought, *'Tis the least I can do. I'll leave this inside with a note.*

Pushing the door fully open, she let herself into a dark and musty-smelling room. A small fire smoldered in the fireplace.

As her eyes adjusted to the darkness, she saw a boy's blond head, facing away from her, his thin body strapped to an upright plank chair.

She moved quickly across the room. "Zebediah?"

The head bobbed erratically as the utterance struggled forth laboriously. Without a doubt, Hannah heard the words "I am."

Hannah didn't hesitate. She unhitched the leather belt and scooped the boy into her arms and took him out into the warm afternoon sun. She held him against her as they sat on the slat-backed bench near the washtubs. She spoke soothingly to him, assuring him she would not hurt him. As he relaxed his body, Hannah was positive he understood. She told him her name and who she was.

"Zebediah, I want to help ya. I want to do somethin' fer ya. 'Tis possible. Perhaps by our tryin' we can figure it out."

Hannah knew that Zebediah was no longer a little boy, but much older than he had first appeared. Even though he was naturally slight of build, it was evident also that he was half starved.

"The first thing I can do, 'tis to feed ya."

She slathered her fresh wheaten bread with churned butter and offered it to Zebediah. It was clear that he was enjoying it by how quickly it disappeared. Next came the pie, and Hannah was certain she saw some life appear in his dull eyes.

Halfway through the pie, Flora arrived.

The look of questioning hostility was apparent. Hannah began a stammering introduction and felt slightly embarrassed by having barged uninvited into their lives.

It was then that Indian Will appeared and startled Flora so much she forgot her anger. Taking advantage of the moment, Hannah composed herself enough to make an offer.

"Miss Floyd, please let me come visit Zebediah. 'Tis difficult fer ya to raise an injured child. He must be lonely. I could come a few times a week. Really, I don't mind. I would like to try to teach him. I can bring food. Surely that would help ya." Then Hannah flashed her warm smile.

Flora thought Hannah a bit crazy. Zeb couldn't learn. His brain was damaged. She looked over at the basket and saw the ham and what remained of the pie. Maybe, just maybe, there was some advantage to the offer.

"Zebediah, I'll see ya late mornin', tomorrow."

With that said, Indian Will and Hannah left quickly before Flora could respond.

Hannah was flushed with excitement as she told Seamus what had happened. How Zeb could speak and understand. She was certain.

Seamus just shook his head. "Hannah, darlin', ya'll be like a fish on dry land. How can he be taught after all these years of bein' strapped to a chair?"

Seamus knew she would try regardless of what he said. He was just happy to have her back home safely.

What no one knew, except Zebediah, was that he didn't sit all day long with a blank mind. He made up stories in his head, saw pictures in the fire, in the grain of the logs, in the swirls of the puncheon floor, and he spoke words that described them. It took huge effort, just one word at a time, but it was what kept him from giving up and dying.

Zebediah liked that pretty brown-haired lady almost as much as the pie.

Underground

In 1858, times were turbulent. The country turned vicious. No one agreed. Brother argued against brother. Mobs seemed to dominate justice. Negroes were owned, sometimes abused. Black women were intimidated, raped, and beaten. Land-Grant Bills that could have opened the West to homesteaders were blocked by Southern politicians who feared a shift in balance of slave-versus-free states. The transcontinental railroad was also stymied. There were raging debates as to whether it should begin in a Northern or Southern city. The country was being ripped apart.

Seamus had seen what prejudice could do. It had haunted him, chased him throughout his life. How could one person ever own another?

'Tis true. Hannah owns me heart, but it be different from the buyin' and sellin' of another person. 'Tis by love, the buildin' up, not by the tearin' down, the free givin' of oneself that makes the blessed saints proud.

But much of the world seemed twisted and angry. Reasonable men and women, in all other areas of their lives, seemed intent on destroying the spirit of those who seemed different or who were without power.

Is there no place on earth where there be all kinds of people treated equally and valued?

Those were the thoughts mulling in Seamus' mind when unexpectedly, Granny Sare appeared at the wood shop door.

"Seamus, I need to talk to ye and yer sweet Hannah."

Granny appeared older. Blue-black wrinkles were deeper around her eyes and mouth. Her hair was now gray. A weariness was etched all over her, even in the way she walked. She had spent the night before in deep, agonizing prayer.

"Lord, you and me gotta have a talk. Git comfortable 'cause I's gonna lay me burden down, right at yer feet. Dem dark roads, dey's gittin' too dark, hard, and cold fer me. I say 'Sare, ye're too old to be doing dis here roamin' and hidin'.' Den I know, ye put it in mah heart to go after dem in bondage. I tries wid all my life and breath to gits them free. But you and me gots a big problem, 'cause I ain't got de strength. Ye gotta make me a young'n agin or show me de way."

Hannah was working at the loom and, hearing Seamus call, came quickly to the shop. Granny began to tell a story of a young woman named Haddie. She and her son, Nicodemus, had escaped from a plantation near Richmond.

Two weeks before, her brother was caught trying to escape. As a lesson to the other slaves, he was bound and placed in a barrel. Sharp spikes were driven into the staves at many angles. The slave master ordered Haddie to push the barrel down a steep hill. Then three male slaves were given the task of rolling it back up and breaking it open to reveal the bloody, mangled body of her brother. The master laughed and warned any attempt to escape would result in such treatment.

It had the opposite effect on Haddie. She knew her son would soon be sold farther south where conditions were even worse. The slave master had made advances toward her. It would be just a matter of time before she would be forced to submit. She vowed to kill herself and her boy before that ever happened. The master had already called her insolent and flogged her thirty times in an attempt to intimidate her.

Haddie fled the same night her brother had been killed, taking Nicodemus with her. They ran by night, waded rivers and streams, and slept in trees.

"Follow the Drinking Gourd, the North Star," she had been told.

The speculators had been offered a five-hundred-dollar reward for their capture and return. They were not far from finding her. She had made it all the way to the South Branch of the Potomac. Word had come to Granny Sare that Haddie and Nicodemus were hidden in a cave near Raven Rock Spring. It was too dangerous for Granny Sare to bring them to her home.

Granny Sare's big eyes, rimmed in red from little sleep, looked to Seamus, then to Hannah.

"'Tis dangerous work ya do, Granny. Guide me to them. We'll bring them here fer a rest. Together with the saints of God, I'll get them to Samuel's church in Cumberland," promised Seamus.

It was unspoken, but the three of them knew that if Seamus were caught, he'd be fined heavily and thrown in jail. Hannah also knew that for Seamus, there was no real choice. No more than she had in going to Zebediah.

Granny cautioned Seamus, "Ye need to be extremely careful. De speculators be everywhere, 'specially in Walnut Bottom below Cumberland. Dey taken it 'pon themselves to search de wagons and even open cargo trunks. Some free blacks ben kidnapped and sold south."

Seamus thought for a while and looked at Hannah.

"Do ya think we could hide them here fer a couple of days? 'Tis the time I need to get ready."

Hannah thought of the twins. They were old enough to understand the seriousness of keeping a secret. She also thought of Haddie and Nicodemus, cold and frightened in the cave.

"There be no other way, Seamus."

Seamus left with Granny in the cool air of the moonless night. Hannah made ready the hiding place in the far back corner of the barn loft. Out of the hay, she made a nest big enough for two.

She fetched wheaten bread from the pantry, butter and apples from the spring house, dried venison strips from the smokehouse, and two warm blankets for the dreamed escape to Canaan Land. Before dawn, Seamus delivered the exhausted slaves to the safety of the warm and fragrant loft.

Early in the day Seamus backed the wagon up to the wood shop door. He measured, sawed, and hammered most the morning, and by noon he was satisfied. He had created a false bottom to the wagon with just enough room for two people to lie flat. Air holes were drilled in the bottom and sides. It wouldn't be comfortable, but Seamus believed that his special cargo could ride through Walnut Bottom undetected.

That evening, with the curtains closed, Hannah, Seamus, Mairéad, Connor, Haddie, and Nicodemus sat around the warming fire and shared their stories.

The twins had always thought of Granny Sare as a close member of the family. They loved the color of her skin. More importantly, they loved the person inside the skin. It never occurred to them that people could be owned, until now.

Folks in the community had come together to rebuild Granny's house after the speculators had burned it down.

She had done so much for so many that people were eager to help.

Connor was grateful for his own story about how she had saved his life when he was born, how she had protected him from evil men when he was hoeing in the garden.

These stories transferred caring and affection over to all who seemed mistreated. Color didn't matter. Now there were the stories from Haddie and Nicodemus that further cemented their beliefs. No one went to sleep that evening without being changed forever. Hatred would never be the dominating force in their lives.

The three left late afternoon the following day. Seamus had tied four chairs onto the wagon bed. If questioned, he would be delivering them to Pennsylvania. He also had next to him the old flintlock. To add to the menacing effect, he pulled off the ribbon that held his unruly red hair. Since the burial of his leg, he had grown back his beard.

Hannah assured him, "Oh, Seamus, 'tis a mighty and wild Celtic warrior ya be. Oisin would look no more fierce. There be no one so foolish as to challenge ya."

Haddie and Nicodemus lay flat on their backs under the false bottom of the wagon. It was uncomfortable but far better than sleeping in trees, fleeing through swamps, and hearing the baying of hounds in the distance.

Seamus pulled into Walnut Bottom just as the sun was setting. Hues of red and gold reflected on the shimmering waters of the Potomac.

The town was jarring to see. It was little more than a crowded camp filled with rough canawlers and railroad workers. Women dressed in gaudy clothes stood by the dirt roads enticing anyone who rode by to sample their delights. Speculators were noticeably present, dressed in their dandy clothes. Taverns and gambling houses did a steady business.

It was a place of lawlessness. No sheriff or any of his men thought it worthy of their time.

People noticed Seamus as he guided his gray through the streets. The wind had blown his hair into a frenzy of tendrils and the fading light glinted off the red locks.

Ahead were a group of six men who had stopped a wagon. They were pulling apart a cargo of woolen goods, letting it drop onto the damp street. The driver was visibly agitated. Finding nothing, the men started to walk toward Seamus.

A stocky man in a brown felt hat reached for the bridle of his gray. Seamus flicked his whip and the man's hat tumbled to the ground.

His green eyes flashed as Seamus declared, "You'll not be touching me horse, nor the chairs I'm deliverin'." He slid his hand toward the flintlock and gently caressed the butt.

The men hesitated, looked in the wagon bed, and a tall, scar-faced man grunted, "Pass by."

Seamus was disappointed. "'Tis a fight I be wantin'."

It had been a long time since he had been in a brawl. He was sure he could have smashed all six heads together. Perhaps it was maturity that made him go on by. After all, he had two runaways in his care. It wasn't his job to turn their present discomfort into danger.

Seamus followed the road up the hill past Emmanuel Church that overlooked the river. Granny had said to hide the wagon in the pine grove a short distance away and wait.

Samuel, the church sexton, would ring the bell on the hour. If it was safe, the bell would hesitate after the third and fifth toll. Steady ringing would mean danger. If it was safe, then the mother and son were to enter by the north side door.

Late in the night, they would be guided to the next stop on the Underground Railroad, north to Pennsylvania, and then finally on to Canada.

The bell tolled three, hesitated, and then tolled on to five, hesitated, and then steadily rang to nine. Seamus pried up three boards from the false wagon bottom. Haddie and Nicodemus slowly and stiffly crawled out, over the edge to the ground.

Haddied rubbed the small of her back and stretched. "Mass'r Seamus, dat be da most unforgettable ride." All three hugged in the dark night.

"May the blessed Bride and the angels in heaven be with ya every step of yer journey," whispered Seamus.

From the shadows, another conductor emerged to lead the runaways to the safety of the tunnels deep beneath the church. For Seamus this would be the first of fourteen deliveries as a conductor of the Underground Railroad.

He arrived home late that night. Hannah and the twins had waited up for him.

"We couldn't sleep. We need to hear everything. Were ya afraid? Are they safe?" chimed all three.

"Hannah, darlin', this evening proves it." He grinned. "'Tis in me heart. I knew I would always be a railroad man."

By Inches

Hannah kept her promise to Zebediah. She went to him three times a week, always keeping to the same days and time. It mattered to her that he trust her. It was important that he could look forward to something good and different in his life.

At first she mainly brought food to him. He was so thin and weak that he had difficulty lifting a spoon to his mouth. His paralysis extended down his right side, rendering his arm and hand useless and his leg unable to support his weight. His left side seemed strong enough but uncoordinated.

Hannah devised a small bag filled with dried beans and corn. The cloth was bright blue rimmed in sunshine yellow, made from an old dress that Mairéad had outgrown. She told Zebediah that it matched his hair and eyes. Zeb thought he had never seen anything prettier.

But it was what they did with the bag that so pleased him. They played catch. First up close. Then gradually, by inches, Hannah stepped farther back.

"Toss it hard, Zebediah. Harder. Hard as ya can," encouraged Hannah.

And over time his left arm became stronger. His aim became better, so much so that he could drop that bag into the empty washtub at ten yards.

It wasn't just the strength she worked on but his words as well. They came out in agonizingly slow, small, contorted explosions. But they came, and Hannah could understand their meaning.

"Bean bag" became his first new words, followed by "blue," "yellow."

Hannah wasn't satisfied with merely teaching him new words to say. She wanted to have Zeb read, if only simple things. She had observed that two words strung together were the most he could say. She'd start there. Large cards with simple two-word sentences was how she introduced the new wonder of reading. "Toss bag." "Eat pie." "Dog bark." "Drink water." The combinations were endless and slowly, with enormous effort, Zebediah learned.

Hannah remembered that the first words Zebediah said were "I am." So she believed that by adding a new word to that, Zebediah could string three words together.

"I am Zeb." "I am cold." "I am hungry." "I am sad." "I am happy."

On and on came new words and concepts. Zebediah was being freed from the body that had held him captive for so many years.

If only I could help him walk, thought Hannah.

He had been pulling himself around by leaning on the back of a chair and sliding it, but that had its limits.

"If Seamus could make a leg, then surely he could fashion a support fer the boy."

"All right, Hannah, darlin', bring him here. I'll be needin' to measure him. Perhaps I can make something that helps, but I'm never goin' to Oldtown." Seamus was emphatic.

It was quite a sight, the old Indian with his hat of turkey feathers, the tousled-blond boy, and the pretty brown-haired lady riding through Oldtown in a wagon, pulled by the large gray horse.

The townspeople had heard from Flora who Hannah was. They also heard how Zebediah could talk and even read. Word had spread and at least some of the villagers conceded that not all Irish were progeny of the devil.

Hannah didn't always have Will with her. She felt safe riding to Zebediah's house, but she was grateful that Will was with her today. Zeb's body had filled out and was taking on the stature of a young man. If he fell, Hannah would have had a difficult time getting him onto the wagon.

As Will pulled the wagon into the barn, Seamus noticed how much Zebediah had changed from that fateful time when he first met the boy. He was bigger. His eyes were not dull. His blond hair no longer looked like dried straw. It shone in the sunlight.

Proudly, slowly, with effort, the young man said, "I am Zeb."

He couldn't help himself. Seamus gave him a big hug, and then an even bigger one to Hannah. He was conscious of the softness of her body. Yet he knew too that the core of her was nothing less than iron.

"Come into me wood shop, Zebediah. 'Tis a lot of work we have to do."

With that said, Seamus supported him on his right side and set him down on a newly finished Windsor chair. The two stayed there until dinnertime.

"'Tis how to do it, Zeb. With yer left hand, place it under yer right arm. Reach over and buckle the harness behind yer neck. Good. Now we will practice. 'Tis what I did before Hannah saw me with me new leg."

Later that afternoon, Hannah, Mairéad, and Connor watched as Zebediah made his way toward the porch. Seamus was close by his side to support him if he lost his balance.

"The hard part, Zeb, will be the steps. Lead with yer left leg. Good."

Seamus steadied him as he made his way to the porch. "With practice ya'll be able to do that by yerself."

Everyone clapped. As they sat down to dinner, Hannah was beaming. Seamus thought about how interwoven lives could be. Strange how paths keep crossing. He loved Hannah. He loved her huge caring heart.

Of course Zebediah was to stay the night. Bedtime had to wait until everyone, including Indian Will, played several rounds of bean bag catch.

The children called Will "Grandfather." Hannah was even teaching Zebediah to do the same. As Will looked around the room, a feeling of great pride swelled inside him. He was very pleased with his new tribe.

Convergence ||

Four years had passed since Hannah first met Zebediah. Much had happened in that time. Mairéad and Connor were now fifteen. They had completed all the education the small one-room school could provide. The teacher had come to visit and urged Hannah and Seamus to send the children away to school in a large city.

"They are bright and need a chance to follow their dreams," she implored. "Mairéad is excellent in science. Perhaps she can be trained to work in one of the large hospitals. Lord knows, they could use the help. Connor has a sharp business sense, and he loves farming. There are new ways of doing things these days. He could bring back good ideas for the Malone homestead."

It hadn't occurred to Seamus that his children were even old enough to think about their future. And to think of leaving home? He didn't even hesitate long enough to look at Hannah. The answer was "No."

It was Mairéad who persuaded him. Hannah's sister, Leah, was recently widowed and lived alone in a large house in

Hagerstown. The train left Patterson Creek regularly and had a stop close to her home.

"It wouldn't be difficult to come home on weekends. Aunt Leah has always said we could stay with her. She never had children. We could try it for a year," chimed the twins.

Well, seeds do sprout. It wasn't but a month gone by before all four of them boarded the train and went to see Leah. Everything fell into place, the schools, the train schedule, and Aunt Leah. September would be the month the twins would leave.

As for Zebediah, his skills slowly improved and some just leveled off. Nothing could restore the damage done by the bullet.

"But what of wholeness? How many people experience life totally unscathed?" Hannah couldn't think of an exception.

She was proud of how far he had come.

The villagers became used to seeing Zebediah and Hannah. Each day when Hannah was there, the walks got a little longer. The stick harnessed to his right side gave him mobility, a dream he had dared never to have. He became so proficient that they both were determined to explore every square foot of Oldtown.

Even Flora's life changed for the better. The parish church hired her on as a maid and cook for their pastor. All that praying finally paid off. Flora was grateful too for Hannah and called her a great healer. Most of the people in town had come to admire Hannah.

In October of 1859, a man named John Brown raided Harper's Ferry Armory and Arsenal. He was captured, tried, and hanged. Some say he just wanted to free slaves, but the violent way he attempted such an uprising didn't make sense to Seamus and Hannah.

They had heard about a man named Abraham Lincoln who might become president and free the slaves. Hopes were so pinned on him that there were dramatically fewer fugitive slaves. It seemed that everyone was waiting to see what would happen.

By November of 1860, Mr. Lincoln was elected president of the United States The world seemed to go crazy. Some viewed him as a new Messiah, others as the devil incarnate.

There seemed to be no middle ground. Sides were chosen, families split. On December 20, 1860, South Carolina seceded from the Union. February 9, 1861, Jefferson Davis became the president of the Confederate States of America.

War was inevitable.

Winter snow came pouring down, coating trees and hills as if to purify the earth, to make ready for the blood-soaked bodies it would receive.

The snow lasted until March, and Hannah had been unable to visit Zebediah. She had hoped to have him stay for a few days over Christmas when Mairéad and Connor were home, but the snow prevented that. Now that the roads were clear enough, Hannah decided to take some belated gifts to him. She wanted him to have the blue and yellow coverlet she had woven especially for him. She also knew that the butter fudge would be well received.

Seamus hitched up the gray to the wagon and made Hannah promise not to stay long.

"Be back by early afternoon before any more snow decides to fall."

He had loved being snowbound with her. His mind drifted back to three weeks ago when the snow had continued to fall. They had stayed in the four-poster bed all morning only to get up briefly to eat. Seamus made the coffee while Hannah toasted the dark wheaten bread over the coals and then slathered the slices with freshly churned butter. When that hunger was sated, they turned their attention to the other hunger.

Under the indigo and rose coverlet, they explored, stroking and carressing the familiar parts of each other. Then Hannah braided his long, now graying beard into three sections.

"Seamus, you look like Poseidon, the terrible Greek god of the ocean," she laughed.

"Then 'tis so, darlin' Hannah. I shall take my trident and plunge deep into the sea."

She shrieked in mock terror. They laughed the entire time of their lovemaking until the powerful orgasmic moment took their breath away.

Now she was leaving on a visit to see Zebediah. It had been a long winter. He couldn't blame her.

"Hannah, darlin', ya be careful and come back to me soon."

"Seamus, I promise."

As the gray pulled the wagon toward Broad Hollow, Seamus again felt that welling up of fear. His pulse thundered in his head.

Why does this keep happenin'? I should know better than to let fear have such a hold on me.

It felt good to Hannah to be out on a short jaunt. People talked about cabin fever. She could hardly wait for spring. She could smell it in the air. There were still patches of snow on the ground in the shaded areas, but the warming sun would take care of that in a couple of weeks.

She looked forward to seeing Zebediah. She missed him and was sure the feeling was mutual.

"I hope he has been practicing his reading."

She had tucked inside the coverlet a children's book about the Christ Child. She was sure Flora would approve. Ever since she began working for the pastor, she had fancied herself a biblical scholar. Hannah smiled. She really missed these people.

Hannah tied the gray to the hitching post and pulled her bundle from off the seat. As she made her way to the steps leading to Zebediah's house, she noticed footprints in the snow where it was shaded. She could tell they weren't Zeb's. There were no stick marks, and they were larger.

"Good. Someone has been here for a visit. I had hoped a friend would look in on Zeb while Flora worked."

She knocked loudly on the door. "Hello, Zeb. 'Tis me, Hannah."

She pushed open the door. It felt so familiar. This was how she always arrived.

The room was darker than usual. All the curtains were drawn, and it took Hannah a while for her eyes to adjust. Strapped to the plank chair, with not one belt but two, was Zebediah.

A look of horror crossed Hannah's face, then anger. "Who did this to you?" She raced to him and quickly unbuckled the belts.

Zebediah looked pale as he struggled to speak. "Go! Go!" he shouted.

But it was too late.

From the back room came barreling a thick-bodied, unshaven man with small feral eyes. His rotting teeth gave off a powerful stench.

There was no doubt in Hannah's mind that this was Jerral. He lunged at Hannah, closing his hands around her neck. She struggled to get away. To get his hands off her, she scratched, dug at his eyes, and pulled on his iron grip. Then with a sudden move she kneed him in the groin. As he moaned loudly, his hands loosened.

Hannah thought she could make it to the door. Jerral bellowed and grabbed her blouse, then her shoulders. With brute strength, he slammed her head against the rock fireplace. Hannah fell to the floor as blood seeped from her smashed skull.

"You Irish bitch," screamed Jerral.

Those were his last words. His eye caught a glint of silver. A large carving knife sailed end over end, through the air, as if in slow motion. He froze in terror as it sliced through his jugular. Jerral slithered to the floor, stunned, his eyes locked on to Zebediah. Blood gushed, drenching the wood beneath him.

Zebediah dragged himself to Hannah and cradled her in his left arm. In their closeness, he could feel her heartbeat, hear her shallow, erratic breathing. Then came the deadening silence.

As Jerral lay dying, he heard his son weep.

Broken

Hannah was late and Seamus was agitated. She had promised to come back soon. His emotions bounced from being annoyed at her for taking so much time, to fretting about icy patches on the road.

What if the wagon slid off into the ditch as she rounded the curve to Broad Hollow?

Relief came over Seamus as he heard the buckboard coming up the path to the cabin. He looked out, but instead of seeing Hannah, he recognized the sheriff with Zebediah seated next to him. Behind, another wagon followed, driven by a priest dressed in black.

That white blinding sensation struck him full tilt and made the room swirl around. He stumbled out the door of the cabin screaming Hannah's name. Behind Zebediah lay Hannah, carefully wrapped in the blue and yellow coverlet.

"God damn me. God damn me stubborn soul. Blessed Mother of God, not me darlin' Hannah. Please, please not me darlin'," Seamus sobbed hysterically.

Inconsolable, Seamus carried her to their carved four-poster bed and lay next to her. He held her body close to his and buried his face in her blood-soaked chocolate hair.

"I won't let ya take her. Take me. Let me life be taken. It can't be. She is too good," cried Seamus.

Indian Will appreared at Hannah's bedside late that evening. His face was painted black. His limbs shone with bear grease in the candlelight. His braided hair was mostly white now with just a few graying strands. He was dressed simply in deerskin trousers and shirt, wore no *kestoweh*. The Indian gently nudged Seamus, who had not moved from the bed since he had laid Hannah's body there. Seamus roused himself and sat on the edge of the bed, holding his face in his hands.

"Seamus, she is no longer here. She is being returned to the earth, our Mother. There will be times when you will still know her. She will be in the gentle breezes, the dew on the grass, the flickering stars above. Do not fear death."

He carefully placed a pillow of beaver fur under her head as a symbol of comfort, harkening back to those many years ago in the cave.

The old Indian then lit bundles of wild hemp, sweetgrass, and sage. He waved the wispy smoke over her body and chanted his sweet Hannah into the care of the Great Spirit.

There was no wake that evening. The unexpected death and the violence that caused it all but stopped the simplest of acts. The family and friends who loved Hannah were in shock.

The earth was still partially frozen and hard to break, but Seamus slammed the pick into the earth over and over until the cold ground gave way. He dug not one but two graves. He felt dead and welcomed the idea of crawling into the grave next to Hannah.

He remembered his promise to her. Nothing would come between them. He would be buried next to her, separating her from that piece of him that had become the symbol of Jerral's hatred. Seamus was too late to protect Hannah from that evil, but he would place his body as a shelter between the two.

As the morning sun warmed the earth, people came. There were long lines of wagons and horses. Many came walking, some even from the train stop at Patterson Creek. It seemed that the entire village of Oldtown was there.

Zebediah stood on the edge of the crowd, leaning heavily on his stick. His whole body shook as tears streamed down his face. Hannah had been the greatest kindness in his life. She had taken his damaged body and freed him from being trapped. She gave him love, speech, and movement. Most importantly, she understood. His heart pounded as he recalled holding her, feeling her heart beat, then stop.

"Too slow. Zeb slow. Too slow," he whispered, punishing himself over and over.

Connor went to him. "Zebediah, ya be one of us now." He guided him to the grave site. Mairéad and Connor held him between themselves.

Seamus was surrounded by his children, his elderly parents, Indian Will, Granny Sare, Hannah's sisters, and awkwardly, the Roman Catholic priest and the Presbyterian minister.

To their credit, each performed his own burial rite, choosing not to discuss the matter at this sad time. Hannah, true to her solution of so many years ago, received a double burial that St. Peter was sure to honor.

Seamus lay on the grave until the cold, turned earth numbed his body. He sent his tears down, down, deep into the ground to his Hannah, darlin'. Mairéad and Connor stood watch until their sadness could stand no more. Then they led Seamus home to the warming fireside.

Indian Will remained. He sat cross-legged at the foot of Hannah's grave and chanted softly, rocking back and forth, until the light of the setting sun faded.

"A-gi-do-da, a-gi-tsi, gv-ge-yu-i Hannah *a-da-ne-di, a-yi-a-wa."*

He seemed to shrivel into the earth as he mourned his Hannah. To him, she had been his own beloved daughter.

Shattered

Seamus woke in the morning, grudgingly. It had to be a terrible nightmare. He could feel her warmth next to him. All he needed to do was to reach over and pull her close. He slid his trembling hand over the blanket, praying he'd find Hannah. But she wasn't there.

He knew. His heart shattered as his mind slowly reconstructed the events of the past few days. He could have stopped her from going to Zebediah's. He should have stopped being stubborn and gone with her to Oldtown. The recriminations tugged at him, driving him down, deeper, into his utter despair.

Mairéad and Connor knew their father wanted to will himself dead. Seamus was even quite capable of taking his own life. The twins had lost one parent and were determined to keep him alive. Both refused to return to Hagerstown to continue schooling. It was just as well, as war was inevitable.

Mairéad faced her father. Her unruly copper hair and green eyes mirrored back to him a young version of himself. Her temper and decisiveness were to be reckoned with.

"I am going to ask Zebediah to live with us. I will continue to teach him as Mum did. I need ya to help."

"'Tis no help I be to anyone, Mairéad," muttered Seamus.

"You could be if ya choose." She glared at him. "'Tis my loss too. All the good done for Zeb is not to be forgotten. The least ya could do would be to take Zeb on walks through the hills and play catch. He needs to keep up his strength."

Seamus hadn't been out of the house except to go to Hannah's grave. He'd sit there stony-faced for hours on end. It made the twins nervous to know where he was. His grave was dug, just waiting for him. Bringing Zebediah home would give them both, Zebediah and Seamus, a reason to live.

The weather warmed and in the evening the peepers began to sing down by the creek bed. Hannah had loved that sound.

As the three sat on the cabin porch, Connor played his mother's dulcimer. When the familiar tune "Barb'ry Allen" merged with the sound of the peepers, Seamus began to sob. Connor, with his dark curly hair, looked remarkably like his mother in the fading light. His music conjured up Hannah's presence. It seemed to each of them that she was there.

Connor spoke softly. "Da, you know what Mum would want ya to do."

Fame

Zebediah did come home with Mairéad and Connor. Flora was relieved to have him taken in by people who cared. It wasn't good for him to sit alone in that room with the bloodstained floor. She had poured on hot water and lye soap, scrubbed hard, but it was still there.

Flora had been as shocked as anyone about Jerral's return to Oldtown. Last she had heard, he was jailed in Martinsburg, sentenced for life.

No one had heard that a mob had set the inmates free, extracting from them the promise that they would fight for the Confederacy.

How could anyone even think he would come back? Flora didn't know that the Pine Tavern owner had sent a message to him about how the Irish woman named Hannah, Shay's wife, was teaching Zebediah. How his very own sister had welcomed her.

Jerral had seethed for two years in his cell. He fully intended to kill Flora, for her deceit, if ever he had the chance. Flora had left for work at the parsonage just minutes before Jerral had arrived hungry and filled with hate.

Seamus tried to do what Hannah would have wanted. He took Zebediah on walks through the hills. People on Dan's Run Road would see them together. The tall, slightly stooped copper-haired man with his peg leg and the slight, yellow-haired young man with his stick. They knew their stories and felt sad.

Yet so remarkable was the story of the brain-damaged boy, his progress with the Irish healer named Hannah, and the tragic deaths that followed that a reporter from the *Cumberland Civilian and Telegraph* newspaper wrote a sensational story about the events in Oldtown. *The Herald of Freedom and Torchlight* in Hagerstown reproduced the story and placed it on the front page next to the ads for Shriner's Balsamic Cough Syrup and Indian Vermifuge. Reports on battles of the war were to be found on pages two and three.

The story spread to Baltimore and then on to Philadelphia. There were a few medical doctors who took notice.

Sympathies

On April 17, 1861, Virginia seceded from the Union. Maryland stayed. It was obvious that war would come close, too close. For the Malone family, it seemed strange that they found themselves living within the boundaries of the Confederacy. The northwestern part of Virginia was, in fact, fairly evenly divided in their sympathies.

In July, at the first battle of Bull Run, the Union army was defeated. Lincoln was quoted as saying, "It's damned bad." He knew the war would be a long one.

Union troops spilled into the Cumberland area and over into Virginia, securing the railroad from the Confederacy. Hospitals were established in Clarysville, Cumberland, and Frederick to receive the sick and wounded.

On September 17, 1862, the Battle of Antietam began by a creek outside Sharpsburg. It ended up as the bloodiest single day in the Civil War. Union forces lost 12,410 men and the Confederates 10,700. There was no decisive victory. In effect, General Lee had failed to take the war into Northern territory. Homes and churches in Hagerstown and the surrounding villages were turned into makeshift hospitals.

Aunt Leah's house was taken over by the Union troops, so she packed a few belongings and left on the first coach to Cumberland. She had decided to stay with the Malones until all this violence was over. Padraig and Dierdre were quite elderly and welcomed her with open arms. They surely could use extra help.

The Clarysville Inn had been a popular stagecoach stop along the National Highway for fifty years. During the Civil War it was transformed into a military hospital surrounded by one-story buildings that housed the sick and wounded. Most of the time, anywhere between one and two thousand soldiers were hospitalized there.

Both Mairéad and Connor, while opposed to the killing and violence, found a way to help with the devastating pain and suffering.

Connor worked as an ambulance wagon driver for the Union troops. He hauled hundreds of injured and ill soldiers from the battlefields to the hospitals in Cumberland and Clarysville. He was especially proud to have brought with him some Confederate soldiers as well.

"'Tis brothers we are in the sight of God." That is what Seamus had told him.

Healing was what Connor wanted for these lonely, scared young men. They were his age, sometimes even younger. It profoundly disturbed him when some died before he even got them to the hospital.

Mairéad found herself in a frustrating situation. She had gone to Clarysville to volunteer as a nurse. In Hagerstown, she had trained at the clinic and had been studying to be a medical aid before the war. This gave her more knowledge and experience than most of the other volunteers.

The hospital was understaffed and desperate for help. But the military commander who oversaw the staff at Clarysville rejected her offer. He dismissed her curtly and pointed to the door. Mairéad, confused, started to leave. But before she reached the door, her temper kicked in.

"I'll not be leaving until ya tell me why. You, yerself, have asked for volunteers. 'Tis here in the paper. I'm more qualified than most." Her eyes sparked and her red hair bounced.

He sat at his desk fiddling with his pen, then said, "Nurses are older women and rarely attractive."

Mairéad stared at him, then thoughtfully said, "A sick or wounded man would not care if I be young. If pleasant I be to behold, then that can only be fer the good. Please give me a week to show ya how helpful I can be."

Mairéad had a way. She was as persuasive as her father.

Truthfully, it was difficult at first for Mairéad. Never before had she seen so many gaping, pus-ridden wounds and terrible, blackening sickness, and in such huge numbers. If the wound didn't kill, then disease most often did. Typhoid fever, dysentery, and diarrhea were common. Of the men who died in the hospital, half were from disease, and the other half were from the wounds. Many suffered long and painfully under the primitive conditions. For them it would have been more merciful to die on the battlefield.

Her resolve, however, remained strong. "This dyin', 'tis not easy fer the young men. 'Tis not easy fer me to watch, but it's where I be. There be no runnin' away."

Mairéad was devoted and dependable. She followed orders, emptied bedpans, changed dressings, and read to those who found comfort in words. In many cases, it was her cooling hand they felt on their brow as death took them from their suffering.

But it was the letters she wrote for the men that made her most proud.

She placed her hand on the young soldier's forehead. "Please continue. You are doin' jist fine. I'm writin' every word jist as ya say it. 'Tis beautiful," encouraged Mairéad.

My Dearest Annie,

With jist a month to go of me hundert days, the Rebels set out to attack the railtown of Cumberland. Our General Kelley proceeded against them. 'Twas jist outside of Folck's Mill, I got shot in the stomach. Annie, the fever is settin' in. The pain is fierce. I believe that death will take me.

Remember those purty flowers I picked fer ya in the mountain field next to our cabin? I called them me Annie flowers. Yeller petals, the color of yer hair, the dark center matching yer eyes. When they bloom, dear Annie, think of me and the love I have fer you. Help young Seth to always remember me. He'll grow strong. I'll live on in him. I wish I had more time to hold you both in me arms again.

Faithfully, with all me love, Davy

Mairéad put the pen down on the crude wooden table beside the dying man. She carefully folded the letter in half, picked up the pen again, and wrote Annie's name and the village town in Pennsylvania where she could be found. She knew the woman was not much older than herself. She probably prayed each night for Davy's safe return.

"'Tis a cruel war," murmured Mairéad.

The latch on the oak box snapped open, and she placed the letter alongside the others. *We're quite a team*, she thought. *Connor is determined to deliver each letter personally jist as soon as the war has ended. Surely he will. 'Tis a deep feelin' he has fer each man he carries to Clarysville Hospital.*

Mairéad turned toward the young man. His last breath had just left him. She reached over and closed his eyes, then pulled the coarse woolen blanket to his chin.

'Tis always a shock, that shell left behind by death, that leavin' of life. Where did the life go? 'Tis me prayer that Davy's soul went to live among those gold-petaled flowers, mused Mairéad.

Head wounds that resulted in paralysis began to show up as the men arrived from the battlefields.

Mairéad told the lead surgeon of her mother's experience with Zebediah. The surgeon had remembered reading the article in the paper. So it was that Mairéad was introduced to the assistant medical inspector for the Union army, Dr. David Mosley.

He was young, lean of body, with black hair and piercing blue eyes. Before joining the Union forces, he had worked at Pennsylvania Hospital in Philadelphia and was involved in research, particularly head trauma and resulting paralysis.

"Mairéad, what more can you tell me about Zeb? Can I meet him?"

And that was how a deeply compatible relationship began for Mairéad and David.

Dr. Mosely was intent that Zebediah should come back with him to Philadelphia. Zeb would have a home there with new friends. His remarkable progress would be studied. A special teacher would be assigned to him so he would be continually challenged to learn. He would be a gift to the medical field, a boon to those many injured in the war.

The family and hospital staff all agreed. There was one abrupt exception. Zebediah said, "No."

I am happy being with Seamus. We are like two broken people who, together, make a whole. At least that was what Zeb thought.

The next day Mairéad took Zebediah on a long walk through the fields. From a distance, Seamus could see Mairéad's flaming hair shining in the sunlight. They stopped a ways off, and she positioned herself squarely in front of him.

With hands on her hips, she said, "Listen to me, Zebediah. You'll not be left alone. Think of all the good."

"Seamus alone," responded Zebediah. "I help."

"Oh, Zeb, ya will come back often. I promise."

The two returned from their walk. Nothing had been settled.

Connor was the next to try the persuasion. He sat Zebediah down on the old bench under the linden tree.

"'Tis not what ya think, us wantin' to git rid of ya. We'll be missing ya. 'Tis what Hannah would want. Ya have so much to give. Remember what it was like before me mum got to ya. There be many so trapped. What would Hannah have ya do?"

Zeb looked at Connor. The man in front of him looked so much like Hannah. His words seemed to come from her. Finally Zebediah agreed.

Seamus was supportive. "'Tis Hannah who'd want ya to go. She would be so proud. Dr. Mosley promises, when this terrible war ends, ya can come back fer visits. 'Tis here yer home will always be."

Three weeks later, David Mosely arranged to take Zebediah to Philadelphia. There had been news from France about Dr. Paul Broca, who had produced a study on neurological damage. It sounded very similar to Zebediah's trauma. The medical community was eager to continue research.

Dr. Mosley arrived at Seamus' home in a covered carriage pulled by a matching pair of bays. After helping Zeb onto his seat and stowing his small bag of belongings, David leaned over and whispered into Mairéad's ear. Ever so gently he kissed her. Mairéad's face turned a lovely shade of pink, and her green eyes sparkled.

Zeb grinned widely. He knew something many of the others did not know.

As the doctor rode away with Zebediah, Mairéad said, "I do think I will be the next to ride away with him."

Seamus gave her a big hug. "'Tis a pleasing thought, Mairéad."

Seamus exhaled long and hard. He was relieved that Zebediah was now gone. He felt that the obligation of caring for him was like two edges of a sword. He loved Zebediah, but he was not the patient teacher that Hannah had been.

'Tis God who knows how hard I tried. 'Tis a great love I have for Zeb, but 'tis the time I need to be alone. Time to mourn.

It seemed that his grief had been put on a shelf when Zeb arrived.

The Waiting

"Oh, me bones, me aching, tired bones." The pain was unrelenting, cutting straight to the marrow.

Granny Sare sat in her twig rocker, in front of the burning embers of the fire. She had padded the seat and back with the sheared hides of two black sheep. One was from her wether, Jacob, the sheep she had used to haul her baskets and yarn along the mountain trails from one small village to the next.

When he died, Granny tanned his thick woolly hide. She nestled into the fleece, and her dark, wrinkled body seemed to disappear. All that could be seen of her in the dim light was the silver curl of her hair as the moon shone through the small cabin window.

In the far distance was the howl of a lone wolf. Standing guard over her penned sheep was Samson, the son of her faithful dog Goliath. The pain of Goliath's death, a long eight years ago, still burned inside. It was as if a sharp claw had torn into her.

She couldn't help herself. Her mind slid back to Hannah's murder.

"Poor chil', to die in such a frightful way was jus' not fair."

But Granny knew the concept of "fair" rarely played out in life, certainly not these days. Just think of Seamus, empty as an old hickory hull, his whole heart yanked out.

Sometimes she could hear the cannons fire. The loud booming bouncing off the hills, echoing through the hollows. Mr. Lincoln's emancipation would come as surely as the fields would be littered with young lives. The hideous price would be paid.

So Granny waited. Her God seemed to insist that she wait, wait until the black angels sang. She was already partway up Jacob's ladder. But each rung was more difficult than the last. Her weary bones pained her as she tenaciously grasped each bar. Soon she'd hear the blessed angels sing. She'd get to the top where there would be no more waiting, no more pain and suffering.

The embers of the fire glowed, casting off a penetrating warmth. Deep sleep came to the old woman wrapped in her memories.

The Stag
1866

Sometimes a man can feel driven, responding to those urges that come from the depths of his being. Perhaps it is primordial, the animal within the soul.

Seamus didn't think much about that gnawing feeling, that powerful need to get moving. He just responded.

It was a late January afternoon. Light snowflakes danced in the gentle breeze, softly landing on the brown earth. He put on his deerskin jacket and the woven cap that Hannah had made. He grabbed the old flintlock and left the cabin.

Perhaps he'd shoot a rabbit in the flats just before the mountain rose steeply. His legs seemed strangely separate from the rest of his body. They carried him in the direction of White Horse Mountain. He hadn't been to the mountain since Hannah was murdered. It had seemed to be a place where only the two of them should go. But it beckoned, pulling him toward it.

Seamus noticed the matted grass, then the large deer tracks. He carefully loaded the rifle. He'd rather have a fine buck than a rabbit. He followed the trail just as the snow began to fall. It fell with a steadiness, covering the ground. As the hoofprints grew fainter under the snow, Seamus realized that they were following the path to White Horse Rock.

He noticed an annoying shortness of breath.

"'Tis me age and me damned peg leg makin' a difference," grumbled Seamus.

The deer prints disappeared shortly before he reached his destination. He placed his gun against a tree and lifted himself onto the stone's flat top. The snow slowed and stopped as darkness fell. The Wolf Moon shone through the scudding clouds.

Seamus felt a peculiar warmth as he sought to catch his breath. The wind sang through the trees. To Seamus it sounded like Hannah's dulcimer, that intoxicating sound that had so many years ago brought him to her.

Looking down toward the river, he saw a sight that he had heard about only in tales. Standing in the clearing was a magnificent stag. Its body was pure white and shone in the moonlight. In a short moment, it was gone.

Seamus laid his head on the cold rock and wept.

"Hannah, darlin', I miss ya so terrible." His chest constricted powerfully from grief.

The snow started to fall again with a ferocity that covered the trees, the land, and all that lay upon the earth.

Epilogue

In the early morning stillness, in an icy white world calmed in the aftermath of a storm, a wizened figure carefully pulled a snow-covered bundle from off the rock. The ancient one lifted the body across his shoulders, seeming to disappear under the burden he carried.

Seamus' body was laid gently on the cabin porch, the old flintlock beside him. The moccasin tracks faded forever beneath the windswept snow.

What's True

This story is true in that, like a Celtic knot design, lives are intertwined with each other and with creation. There is no separation.

There are places that are factual and provided the intrigue and impetus for writing this story.

The graves exist. Except for the descending ridge of Lane Hill, I would be able to see, from my mountain home, the graveyard on the knoll with the long one and the short one beside. The farmer really did say to find the short grave next to the long one. "It's not what you'd think."

The seven graves overlooking the river and the train tracks are as described. I have kicked back the fall leaves in search of them.

Of course the Paw Paw Tunnel is still there. I love to walk through it without a flashlight, fingering my way along the rail, carressing the grooves worn smooth by the mule-pulled ropes.

Oldtown, Maryland, has a wealth of history with caring people, none of whom are like Jerral Floyd. It is possible to drive across the one-lane wooden bridge over the Potomac

River, near the great Warrior Path and ford that Seamus crossed.

The town of Frankfort where the Stone Hotel was still exists. Today it is called Fort Ashby, West Virginia. It is named after a 1755 French and Indian War fort. There is also a historic log building that is a delightful museum owned and managed by the Fort Ashby Chapter of the Daughters of the American Revolution.

The Old Stone Hotel was unfortunately torn down in 1982. But like the phoenix, it took on new life. My husband and I used much of the rock and timbers to build a large stone dining room. Good times of laughter and toasting still bounce off those venerable rocks.

Broad Hollow, a winding dirt road, is the path that I travel from home to the village. It is impossible for my imagination not to take me away down barely visible lanes that once led to cabins and farms.

On Dan's Run Road is a farm of shape-shifting, rolling hills made so as light dances across the fields. A remnant foundation, part of the Malone family farm, still remains.

There was an Indian Will. He is a shadowy figure. It is said he lived in a cave. He left an indelible mark on the landscape. A mountain and a creek are named after him.

Many of the locals know that River Mountain is really named White Horse Mountain. It is said to be named after a white rock in the shape of a horse. I have never seen it. So if there is anyone who knows where it is, please take me.

The Underground Railroad was active in Virginia and Maryland. The Sexton Samuel at Emmanuel Episcopal Church, Cumberland, is said to have been a part of the Underground.

The one-hundred-pound "John Davis" maul was in the brickyard at Mount Savage during the 1950s.

Dr. Paul Broca wrote a neurological study in 1861 about a particular head trauma. It became known as Broca's Aphasia.

Acknowledgments

This story would never have been written if my younger sister, Sheryl Robinson, hadn't challenged me to do so. Standing beside the graves, neither of us expected such a rich and complex cast of characters to emerge.

Gratitude also goes to Butch Robinson for his comments and enthusiasm as Sheryl and he pored over my many drafts, adding significant editorial suggestions.

If our good neighbors Dale and Sue Beam hadn't told us the story of the short grave, I would never have given it a thought.

Thanks also to Mary Lou and Darrel Wagoner for showing me the seven graves on the bluff overlooking the tracks and for giving me my first taste of ramps and morrells.

Thanks to Randy Moreland, who told me the story of White Horse Mountain and to Dr. Brian Cauley for our discussions on head trauma, leading me to an understanding of Broca's Aphasia.

Norma Blacke Bourdeau greatly influenced my using Irish and Negro dialect and encouraged, with her visions, a more visceral approach to the story. She, along with Christopher

Kent, Jim Burns, and Sandra Markus, were invaluable in encouraging me to incorporate passion and grit into the characters. They broadened the writing field significantly.

Much appreciation goes to Linda Busken Jergens and Andrew MacAoidh Jergens who helped to proof the original manuscript and to Pamela Wynfield, who with her Navy skills, proofed the final version.

Thanks to James Rada for his encouragement and comments.

My husband, Martin, was profoundly helpful as my major editor, pushing me into depths of exploration and encouraging me to keep working. The characters in this book became our friends.

Finally the Muse of the Potomac Highlands has been delightful to know. She has led me down unexpected paths where voices emerge from the hollows.